Until the Dawn's Light

Aharon Appelfeld

**TRANSLATED FROM THE HEBREW BY
JEFFREY M. GREEN**

Schocken Books, New York

Translation copyright © 2011 by Schocken Books, a division of Random House, Inc.

All rights reserved. Published in the United States by Schocken Books, a division of Random House, Inc., New York, and in Canada by Random House of Canada Limited, Toronto. Originally published in Israel as *Ad Sheya'aleh Amud Hashachar* by Keter Publishing House Ltd., Jerusalem, in 1995. Copyright © 1995 by Aharon Appelfeld and Keter Publishing House Ltd.

Schocken Books and colophon are registered trademarks of Random House, Inc.

Library of Congress Cataloging-in-Publication Data
Appelfeld, Aron.
['Ad she-ya'aleh 'amud ha-shahar. English]
Until the dawn's light / Aharon Appelfeld ; translated by Jeffrey M. Green.
p. cm.
ISBN 978-0-8052-4179-2

1. Jews—Austria—Fiction. 2. Austria—History—1867–1918—Fiction. 3. Jewish fiction. I. Green, Yaacov Jeffrey. II. Title.
PJ5054.A755A6313 2011   892.4'36—dc22   2011007286

www.schocken.com

Jacket photograph © Pete Turner/Getty Images
Jacket design by Linda Huang
Book design by M. Kristen Bearse

Printed in the United States of America
First American Edition
2 4 6 8 9 7 5 3 1

Until the Dawn's Light

I

THEY MOVED FROM train to train, sped past little stations, stopped at level crossings, and set out again with a rush across broad, flat expanses. It all transpired quickly and with frightening precision, as though they were no longer their own masters but in the hands of the railways, which treated them mercifully and moved them from place to place, almost without pain.

Otto was already four, and his mother regarded him as a big boy. She spoke to him and explained things to him that he certainly couldn't understand. Her long and convoluted sentences perplexed him, but Blanca was sure he grasped her intention, and she would go on and burden him with more words. True, Otto asked pertinent questions, not because he understood what was happening, but because he was frightfully logical. Blanca, who was proud of his consistent thinking, was afraid now that he would trip her up. To distract him, she told him about things that never were, toyed with his limited memory, and promised him that before long they would get to a magical place.

"Where are we going, Mama?" he kept asking.

"To the north."

"Is it far from here?"

"Not very."

"Is the north in the country or in the city?"

"The north is up above, my dear."

In her heart she knew she mustn't lie; the boy was sensitive to contradictions. Still, she deceived him, distracted him, and concealed information. Even worse: she made him promises she couldn't keep. Thus she became the accomplice of the speeding trains: together they confused him.

After a week of displacements, Otto stopped pestering her. He slept and barely poked his head out of his coat. Blanca was upset: perhaps his dreams were showing him what she wanted to keep from his sight. She thought that despite her efforts he had figured something out, and that the dream would turn his guess into a certainty—the thought disturbed her. She buried her face in her hands, the way her mother had done when headaches assailed her.

Otto sank ever deeper into sleep, and his face was relaxed. What she would do, and where the trains would lead them, Blanca still didn't know. The summer light was full. The sky was blue, and the fields were yellow and spread out over the low hills. The bright view brought to mind the long vacations she had taken with her parents. They were so far away now, it was as if those vacations had never taken place.

When Otto woke from his sleep he was pale, and he immediately started vomiting. In his infancy he used to vomit, but since then he hadn't complained about stomachaches or vomited. Now he shuddered in her arms as if fleeing from a nightmare.

"We'll get off here," said Blanca, and they got off right away.

It was a small village, with wooden houses scattered amid greenery.

"This is it," she said, as if they had reached a safe haven.

"And there's a river here, Mama." Otto opened his eyes wide.

"I assume so, dear," she guessed, not knowing if she was right. Not far from the station the famous Dessel River flowed energetically. Its clear, gushing waters were well-known.

"Mama!" Otto shouted in astonishment.

"What?"

"Let's go rowing on the river."

The word "river," which Otto pronounced very sweetly, moved her, and she hugged him and kissed him on the forehead. A house for rent was easily found, a little wooden house overlooking the river, wrapped in vines and willows, far from the main road. Inside, darkness reigned, and dried herbs perfumed the air. The landlady, a pleasant-looking elderly woman, said, "Enjoy yourselves. This was my house once. Since my husband's death, I've been living with my daughter."

"When did your husband die?" Blanca asked.

"Two years ago. At the end of June it will be two years."

"I'm sorry."

"That's how it is. What can I do?"

After showing them the secrets of the house, the old woman asked, "And where are you from?"

"From Vienna," Blanca lied.

"God Almighty," said the woman. "All during my youth I wanted to go to Vienna."

"And you never got there?"

"Just once, for an operation."

"Happiness doesn't dwell where we imagine it." Blanca repeated what her mother used to say.

"How true," said the old woman, and she turned to go. She had cultivated a vegetable garden next to the house, and she placed it, too, at her tenants' disposal.

"You can pick to your heart's content."

"Thank you," said Blanca. She was so moved that she hugged the old woman.

Thus the dizziness was halted for a moment. They got up early, ate breakfast, and went down to the river. The river, they found, actually didn't rush. It flowed, slow and clear, and carp swam lazily at the bottom, as though to avoid the danger awaiting them up above. Blanca and Otto swam together for hours, sometimes until sunset. Blanca, finding she could easily buy dairy products from the neighbors, filled the pantry with good food, and at night they would split open a watermelon, sitting and chatting until Otto collapsed on the mat and fell asleep.

But, finally, the blow fell.

"Mama!"

"What?"

"Where's Papa?"

True, she had expected it, but her tongue cleaved to her palate. *Why are you pestering me?* she almost said. But she quickly recovered and murmured, "He'll surely come."

"Here?"

"I'm doubtful that he'll come here, though."

"What's 'doubtful'?"

"It's a promise, dear."

Otto's sensitivity to words always scared her. Other children, she had noticed, also asked the meaning of a word, but Otto's questions had the sharpness of a razor.

"Nobody knows what those darling creatures are capable of." She remembered her grandmother Carole saying that.

Three weeks ago, or, more precisely, seventeen days ago, Blanca had fled with Otto. Since then: running, yearning, and frightening joy. She didn't reveal a thing to him. During the last nights at home, before going to sleep, she had promised him that soon they would cruise down rivers, climb high mountains, and buy ice cream at stands. Night after night, she would secretly share her fantasies with him. With Adolf she had behaved differently, obeying him like a beast, and when he came home from work in the evening, she would serve him his supper without a word. The obedience made no impression on him. If something didn't please him, he'd throw it away. Blanca didn't ask questions or argue. She kept repeating to herself that there were things it was worth bearing shame for.

Blanca had met Adolf in high school. He was a solid, handsome lad, but not an outstanding student. The teachers liked him because of his strength and childlike appearance. Blanca married him in haste, after she graduated. Her parents weren't pleased, but they didn't meddle. Only Carole, her mother's mother, hearing about her marriage to a gentile, didn't restrain herself. Grandma Carole was a simple woman, hardy and irritable. If she didn't like something, she condemned it, and if people annoyed her, she cursed them. She made allowances for no one. Confident in her beliefs, she would sometimes say things that shocked the family. Years earlier, when another of her granddaughters married a gentile, she had said, "A daughter of Israel who shows contempt for the Torah won't live long. The Torah was given to us to observe, not to hold in contempt. God in heaven sees everything and knows everything and won't forgive." That was before she went blind. After that, she became even more zealous. All the family's ups and downs reached her ears; she missed nothing. And when something seemed wrong to her, she would repeat, "The Torah was given to the Jews so they could observe it, not so they'd hold it in contempt." Everybody expected her to die, but for some reason death didn't claim her. After she went blind, her other senses grew keener and her reactions were sharper. She would make her pronouncements with fierce vehemence, sometimes coarsely, and rather than shaming, her words caused pain.

"Slut," she hissed, when she learned of Blanca's marriage.

2

DAY BY DAY the light grew stronger, and red poppies covered the riverbank. The sight of the flowers reminded Blanca of summer vacations when she was Otto's age and her parents were young. Even then the fear of death would assail her in the middle of the day. She kept this a secret and told no one. Sometimes, before going to sleep, she would ask her mother not to put out the light. Her mother, a thin and fragile woman, used to whisper, "There's nothing to be afraid of, dear; darkness isn't anything, just a color. At your age it's not fitting to sleep with the light on."

In time Blanca confessed: "I'm afraid."

"These are just momentary fears, dear. They'll pass very quickly."

Later, the fear of death left her, but another fear came to dwell in its place, a fear of people. Blanca would hide in the closet or under her bed, and Johanna, the housekeeper, would get down on her knees and whisper, "Where's my squirrel, where's my sweet child?" Hearing her whisper, Blanca would chuckle and emerge from her hiding place.

Then Blanca's mother fell ill. She was just thirty-five, and Blanca was still a young girl. For years they dragged her from sanitarium to sanitarium, from doctor to doctor. She would return from those trips wan and pale, her eyes sunken into their sockets, an involuntary smile trembling on her lips. Blanca wasn't allowed to go into her room. She would stand in the doorway and stare at her.

"How are you feeling, dear?" Her mother would address her as though she were no longer in this world.

"Fine, Mama."

"And how's school?"

"I got 'Excellent' on my arithmetic homework."

Upon hearing those words, her mother would close her eyes and spread her hands on the white sheet.

After a while Blanca's mother no longer returned home, except for short intervals. During vacations, Blanca and her father used to go to the mountains to visit her. Those hasty visits, once in the winter and once in the summer, were seared in her memory with burning clarity. In the summer, her father would rent a room near the sanitarium, and they would visit her mother together twice a day. On warm days, her mother would get out of bed, and they would sit in the garden. Blanca noticed that the flower beds were well tended and the grass was trimmed. Sometimes Blanca would show her mother her notebooks. They were neat, and the teacher's "Excellent" sparkled in them.

Blanca's father was a tall, thin man of few words. He would answer all of Blanca's questions distractedly. "True, you're right," he would say. He made his living from a stationery store, which he and a cousin ran as partners. The cousin, Dachs, a fun-loving bachelor, was his total opposite. Whenever they were together, they quarreled. More than once they were about to sell the store and dissolve the partnership, but at the last minute they would make up, and everything reverted to the old order. So it was for years. Blanca's father hated the store, and his face expressed that hatred. With every passing year his face grew more wizened.

Grandma Carole didn't like Blanca's father. She used to say that all the evils that had befallen her daughter were only because of him. Once, when Blanca was five, Grandma Carole spoke harshly to him about his squandered inheritance and about the way he neglected the store and didn't support his family. Blanca's father sat in an armchair and didn't utter a word as Grandma Carole stood there and listed transgression after transgression. Finally he rose to his feet and, shouting louder than she had ever heard anyone shout, said, "Get out of here, you witch!" Grandma Carole responded in an even more terrifying way: she stretched out her neck and screamed, "Here's my throat. Cut it!"

For a long time after that episode, Blanca was not at ease in her father's company. Her mother tried to make her forget that dreadful episode, saying that it was only a momentary outburst. Papa was a good man, she said, one who liked people, and he wouldn't hurt a fly.

3

"MAMA!" OTTO CRIED OUT.

"What, dear?"

"How old are you?"

"Twenty-three."

"So old?"

Blanca laughed, hugged him, and kissed his head.

They'd been living in this enchanted dwelling for a week now. The low ceiling was held up by thick wooden beams. The windows in the rooms were long and narrow, except for the kitchen window; it was broad and protruded outward, bringing the garden and the river inside. During the long afternoon hours, Blanca sat in the kitchen and happily surveyed all the silent things surrounding her. When she stood up, she felt heavy, and her legs wouldn't take her far.

At that hour Otto would be bent over his treasures, moving them from place to place. Every day he brought pebbles, dry branches, and shells home from the river. He would place them in baskets that were scattered about the house. Later, he would gather them around him. Blanca didn't disturb him. She let him immerse himself in his magic. Sometimes he would get tired in the middle of some enchantment, sink down, and go to sleep. When the darkness fell, she would pick him up in her arms and lay him on the broad bed.

It was summer, and the sunset glowed until late at night. Sometimes, for reasons that Blanca didn't understand, Otto would put aside his magical toys and come to sit at her side. Blanca would split open a watermelon or rinse a plate of cherries, and they would eat them together. The evening light would crown his forehead and eyes. His questions were many, little expressions of astonishment.

"Why did the Jews kill Jesus?" he asked one evening, surprising her.

"Who told you that nonsense?" The question made Blanca jump up.

"Aunt Brunhilde."

"It's absolute nonsense. As for Aunt Brunhilde, she's a bitter, fanatical woman who thinks that anything that isn't Christian is worthless. Fanaticism is despicable, and we must always condemn it. Everyone should live according to his own faith, and nobody should criticize someone else's life. You understand me, dear, right?"

Blanca didn't usually raise her voice. Her patience with Otto was limitless. She listened to his questions attentively and only made comments that would enlarge his mind. But this time his question annoyed her. Otto was surprised by her reaction.

"I'm sorry," he said, and hung his head.

"Forgive me, dear," Blanca said. "But there are things that one mustn't pass over in silence. What Aunt Brunhilde told you is a lie, and we can't keep quiet about it. You can forgive a little lie, but you have to raise your voice and protest against a big lie. We can't be afraid. Truth comes before fear. Do you understand me?"

Otto didn't understand her torrent of words and didn't know what to say.

The days were transparent, like the waters of the Dessel, and Blanca's short life now seemed long to her, having been joined to another, unfamiliar life. Sometimes it seemed to her that she had always been drawn to this place, and now that she had finally arrived, she would not soon leave.

"You know, dear, that your mother is a Jewish woman," said Blanca, and immediately felt that a boulder had been rolled off her heart.

"That's very surprising, Mama."

"Why?"

"I thought Jews were different."

"How?"

"I don't know."

Blanca sat in the armchair, and Otto sat opposite her in the rocking chair. He sat straight, and his eyes were full of wonder.

"Are you sorry?" she said.

"I don't want to think about it," he said, and looked right into her eyes.

The evening darkness slowly descended, the heat dissipated, and a moist breeze rose from the water. It seemed to Blanca that she had not done well to reveal the secret to him, and she was about to say, *I was only joking*, but she realized that what was done could not be undone.

Later, they strolled along the riverbank. The water was already dark, but it looked calm. After a summer day full of activity, tranquillity settled on the bushes and the wild grass. Blanca and Otto walked silently. Blanca wanted to say something, but the words slipped away from her. Tension gripped her neck and stomach. Later, when they sat on the mat and Blanca cut a watermelon into cubes, she still didn't know what to say. Finally, she spoke.

"Otto."

"What, Mama?"

"Nothing."

Thus the day fell away. The darkness was thick, and it seeped into the house through the narrow windows.

4

BLANCA HAD CONVERTED to Christianity and married hastily, to avoid watching her mother's prolonged death from up close. Somehow she believed that with this act her fear of death would be lifted from her heart and her mother would be saved. And indeed, that was what seemed to happen: her mother recovered and rose from her sickbed. Her father rented a carriage, and together they all rode to Saint Paul's Church. Blanca's conversion ceremony was long, full of music and prayer. Her parents sat at her side and smiled throughout the service. Although her parents seemed to be content, repressed dread, which hadn't perturbed Blanca for years, returned to her with great force. She trembled as she stood in the church, and she couldn't stop, even after the ceremony was finished and her mother hugged and kissed her. In addition to her parents, some of her school friends had come, too. It seemed to Blanca that she had found the examination difficult, and that there were two questions she hadn't answered correctly. She grasped her mother's hand, as she had done as child when sudden darkness fell upon the house.

A week after her conversion, Blanca married Adolf. Her mother wore makeup and a flowered dress, and she served cakes to the guests. Her father looked young in his white suit, and he chatted happily with everyone, as though he'd been saved from a bad business deal. The wedding lasted for many hours. Adolf's brothers and sisters drank, sang, and danced. At first Blanca danced, too, but after a few rounds she felt dizzy and sat down next to her mother. This was the kind of wedding she hadn't seen before: vulgar and merry. She watched the dancers as though it weren't her wedding but one she'd been invited to. Her father, who had had a few drinks, felt dizzy, too, and sat down next to his wife. His long face turned gloomy. But Blanca's mother didn't stop smiling, as though she were constantly seeing new marvels.

"Very beautiful," she said, as tears flowed from her eyes.

Right after the wedding, her mother's health deteriorated again. She stumbled several times, and headaches constantly plagued her. Blanca came to visit her every day. At first Adolf would join her, but after a while he stopped.

"A patient needs rest," he would say, "and you shouldn't disturb her too much." His words sounded clear and convincing. It seemed to Blanca, too, that she should visit less often.

Despite the depressions that sometimes afflicted her, Blanca was happy. She and Adolf lived outside the city, in a small house surrounded by open fields and the sky.

Blanca's house wasn't far from where Grandma Carole lived. Blanca would give her grandmother's house a wide berth, but, as though in spite, her grandmother ran into her. The blind woman used to trudge through the streets, appearing in places where one wouldn't expect to find her, her head stretched forward, her sealed eyelids twitching and tense. When she sensed that Blanca was near, she would immediately stop and proclaim, "Woe to the converts to Christianity who have forgotten their ancestry and their good fathers, who have exchanged a great faith for belief in wood and stones."

Blanca's mother's illness became more severe, and Blanca avoided visiting her in the afternoon so she wouldn't meet Grandma Carole. Her grandmother didn't hold her tongue, even at her sick daughter's bedside.

"Everybody's converting." Blanca's mother tried to defend her daughter.

"It's a foul deed." The answer came quickly.

"Even respectable Jews are converting today."

"We don't live by their word."

Around that time, the town's rabbi died, and because there were no longer any worshippers, they closed the synagogue. At the rabbi's funeral several wealthy merchants vowed to preserve the house of prayer, but after a while they changed their minds and agreed that it would be best to send the Torah scrolls and the curtain that hung in front of the Holy Ark to Vienna and to close the place. As it happened, the synagogue refused to be ignored. It stood at the edge of the market square, and Grandma Carole would go there every day, stand in front of the closed doors, and proclaim, "Woe to the Jews who have abandoned their Temple. God in heaven will not forgive them, and when the time comes, He will pass judgment on them." The town's Jews dreaded her, and they all awaited her death. But Grandma Carole showed no signs of weakness. On the contrary, ever since she'd gone blind, her voice had become clear and cutting, and she phrased her words simply and clearly. Even her curses had a thundering rhythm.

In the end, the police arrested her.

"Woe to the Jews who deny their Father in heaven," she proclaimed in court. "Those who close a synagogue are closing the gates of prayer." She named the wealthy merchants who refused to pay the janitor's wages. "And for that," she said, "they shall not be absolved. The earth will open its mouth and swallow them like Korach and his followers." When the judge admonished her, telling her that she had to stay in the house and not wander in the street and insult people, she replied, "There is a height above all height, and only that must we heed."

The court released her, ordering the family to keep her from roaming the streets. And the next day, she stood in the synagogue doorway again, calling out the names of the town's Jewish converts to Christianity and wishing that they all would go to hell.

Meanwhile, Blanca's mother's illness grew more severe, and the doctors ordered her to return to the mountains. Blanca wanted to travel with her, but Adolf forbade it.

"You'll end up catching it, too," he said in a tone of disgust. Blanca was frightened, but she didn't disobey him. A day before her departure, Blanca's mother broke down and wept, asking her family for forgiveness for the trouble she was causing. Blanca's father scolded her in a strange manner, and she stopped crying.

Two weeks later a postcard came.

"The Lauter Rest Home received the veteran patient cordially," her father wrote. "The patient has recovered from the trip, and now she is resting in her room. The weather is pleasant, and the apple trees are in full bloom." Blanca reread the postcard several times. The sentence "The Lauter Rest Home received the veteran patient cordially" moved her, and she felt a stabbing in her heart.

Forced by Adolf to neglect her mother, Blanca felt numb inside— heavy, unclean, and weak-kneed. But she still worked day and night to clean the house and put everything in order. She was angry because she had given in to Adolf, and she was overcome with remorse. In the evening, when Adolf returned from work, she didn't tell him about the postcard. Adolf was hungry, and Blanca served him dish after dish.

5

THE SECOND COMMUNICATION from Blanca's father, a long and disjointed letter, arrived a month later. He tried to conceal his distress, but every word in his letter screamed *It's hard for me to bear this alone.* Blanca decided on the spot: *I'm going tomorrow, no matter what.* In the evening, after supper, she told Adolf that her mother's condition had worsened and that she had to go to be with her.

"When?"

"Tomorrow."

"I understand."

"What can I do?"

Only now did Blanca notice how much Adolf had changed over the last few months. His face had gotten fat, and his walk was heavy, like that of a career soldier. He spoke slowly and emphatically, as though to keep the words from slipping. Every utterance pierced her like a nail. At first he didn't blame Blanca but criticized her grandmother Carole.

"She's insane," he would say. Or, "She's a crazy Jewess." Later on he would add, "She passed her madness on to her descendants. Some of them are sick, and some are crazy." Before long he stopped hedging.

"Don't be like her," he would say. "It drives me crazy." Blanca didn't contradict him. On the contrary, it seemed to her that this healthy, strong man had the right attitude toward life and that one day she, too, would be like him. Before leaving for work he said,

"If you want to go to your mother, I won't stop you. But you ought to know that with us, the husband comes before everything else."

The threat was clear, but Blanca interpreted it as passing anger and tried to mollify him. On the train she drank two mugs of beer, felt dizzy, and blamed herself for responding so easily to the desires of her heart and not fulfilling her duty toward Adolf. Later she fell asleep and awoke feeling that she was choking.

When she reached the rest home, Blanca saw with her own eyes how ill her mother was. Her father stood next to the bed, bent over and exhausted, as if he were about to sink to the floor. Blanca, who wanted to know everything about her mother's condition, was choked with sorrow. Later that day her father told her he had already spent the money he had received from his partner for his half of the store, and now he had no choice but to sell the house. *What are you thinking about, Papa?* she was about to say, but she immediately saw the foolishness of it.

The owner of the rest home, a Jewish woman with a warm and gentle expression, received Blanca like a mother. For supper she served them cheese dumplings and borscht with sour cream.

"Thank you, Mrs. Lauter," Blanca said, inclining her head.

"If only I could be more helpful." The woman spoke in the old Jewish way.

In the evening Blanca sat by her father's side and tried to give him encouragement. He was racked with guilt, saying that he hadn't done enough to get his wife to a Dr. Birger, in Vienna. Dr. Birger was known as a miracle worker, but for his miracles he demanded exorbitant sums.

If it weren't for the local doctors, who claimed that Dr. Birger was a charlatan and his medicines were snake oil, he would have sold the house long ago. Now remorse gnawed at his heart.

When they went back to visit her mother, she opened her eyes and asked, "How is Adolf?"

"He's fine," said Blanca. She was angry that, of all people, her mother had remembered Adolf, but she quickly overcame her anger and told her mother about their house, about the new furniture they had bought, and about the carpet, which covered most of the living-room floor, that Adolf had bought in a nearby village. She knew those purchases would make her mother happy.

"Adolf's a good fellow," her mother said.

"That's true," Blanca replied, so as not to leave her mother's sentence with no response.

The doctor who came to examine the patient the following day didn't raise their hopes.

"What can I do?" Blanca's father rose to his feet. "You can't let a person wallow in agony. Why can't we try Dr. Birger's methods?"

The doctor lowered his head, as if to say, *One mustn't delude people,* but her father, who was seized with dread, spoke in a trembling voice about the duty to do everything in our ability to foil death's plots against innocent people.

"If you want to go there, I can't stop you," said the doctor softly. "But it's my duty to tell you that Dr. Birger's methods have no scientific basis, and there's no difference between him and charlatans."

"So we shouldn't go to him?" Blanca's father asked, his eyes closed.

"I didn't say that."

"What should we do, Doctor?"

"In a moment I'll give Ida an injection to ease her pain."

"An injection will ease her pain?"

"It will ease it," said the doctor, and set right to work.

Blanca had thought she would be returning home the next day, but seeing her father bent over and shriveled in his fear, she didn't dare tell him so.

"Papa, why don't you shave, put on a suit, and we'll go out to a café," she said a bit later. Her father did as Blanca asked. In the café, he spoke about her mother's illness, about the store, and about his cousin Dachs, who had cheated and completely impoverished him. And he spoke about not having emigrated to America. If he'd emigrated, his situation would be entirely different. Blanca knew those were merely wishes and fantasies, but she didn't stop him. She let him indulge himself.

That night she saw how her father had aged. That tall man, who was only forty-eight, looked like someone whose flesh had been trampled, whose spirit had been stifled, and who had been seated on the threshold of a world devoid of mercy. True, he was not a practical man; he had squandered his inheritance and he had run the store negligently. But he'd done no harm to anyone. When he expressed wonder or asked a question, he was like a child who makes everyone happy with his inventions. And his wife adored him.

At the railroad station Blanca's father burst into tears, and Blanca, who was astonished by his weeping, hugged him softly.

"It's all right, Papa," she said. "We'll do everything we can to see Dr. Birger."

"Thank you from the depths of my heart," he said, as if she weren't his daughter.

"We will spare neither money nor effort, Papa." The words left her mouth and, amazingly, they calmed him.

"Pardon me, dear, for being so weak," he said.

6

WHEN SHE RETURNED home that afternoon, Blanca found the kitchen in a mess, the beds unmade, and empty beer bottles on the coffee table in the living room. The smell of liquor and cigarettes mingled thickly in the air. Adolf's powerful presence permeated the entire house.

Blanca overcame her immobility. She opened the windows, beat the carpets, and then sank into the dishes that were piled in the sink. The work erased the image of the rest home from her mind, and as she stood in the center of the living room she wondered, *When did I first get to know Adolf well?* It was as though she had suddenly lost her grip on time. Then she remembered a long, lovely summer some years earlier. Nothing out of the ordinary had occurred, but it had been wonderful just the same. Her mother had packed the suitcases because her father was burdened with the store that he despised. Blanca celebrated inwardly. The grades on her report card were splendid: excellent, excellent, and excellent. Her father's joy had been unbounded. His only child excelled not only in mathematics, but also in Latin. In two weeks they would be going north, to the pleasant, cool tributaries of the Danube. Blanca loved her parents, and her affection for them rose and swelled when they were at the river's edge. She loved her father because he was unlike other fathers, and her mother because she imbued her with tranquillity and faith.

In prior years they had gone on vacation to Feuerberg, but more recently they traveled as far north as the unspoiled Winterweiss, where branches of the Danube flowed in broad, silent valleys. In

Winterweiss there were no Jews; the Jews who had converted tried to behave like Austrians, and the Austrians behaved like Austrians. Blanca's father didn't like the company of Jews.

"The Jews have lost their essence," he used to say, "and their emptiness is annoying." His usual soft expression would change when he spoke about his brethren.

When he was young Blanca's father wanted to convert, but his mother, who didn't observe the traditions but was very devoted to her family, forbade it and made him swear that he would not. At first he planned to ignore the oath, but when he realized how much it would pain her, he abandoned the idea. For years he had regretted that.

"If I'd converted to Christianity," he used to say, "my life would have been different."

His wife didn't agree with him. "The Jews are no worse than other people," she would reply.

Blanca's father stuck to his opinion. "They are worse."

Those of his friends who had converted had graduated from the university and done better than he. Some of them were physicians, attorneys, and industrialists, and he barely could support his family. He attributed all his failures to his Jewishness. Jewishness was an illness that had to be uprooted. That brutal statement didn't go with his soft temperament. Nevertheless, he repeated it regularly. In Winterweiss he was at ease. He swam in the river, solved chess problems, read mathematics books eagerly, and if there was a piano, he would play it. That was the father Blanca loved, affable and overflowing with humor.

A week before the end of the school year, three weeks before Blanca and her parents left for Winterweiss, Blanca met Adolf near the school laboratory, and they spoke for a few minutes. Adolf's words had no special content, but they struck her heart; it was as though he had whispered a secret to her. After that, he never left her sight. Adolf wasn't an outstanding student, but the teachers were fond of him because of his height and strength, and they didn't fail him. Even the tall teachers looked short next to him. They saw him as a phenomenon of nature, sometimes saying, "Adolf will pick that up. Only Adolf can do it." Once, he lifted a teacher's desk up on his shoulders, and everyone cheered him. On the playing field, he wasn't one of the swifter athletes, but his strength stood him in good stead there, too. The girls admired him but were afraid of him. Sometimes, when he managed to overcome a mathematics problem, a wild smile would spread across his face, like that of an animal whose hunger was satisfied.

Adolf wasn't particularly kindhearted, but he was always ready to help carry building materials or move cabinets. In the spring he would help the gardeners, and if a boy got hurt, he would carry him to the infirmary in his arms. He was a friend of the principal and assistant principal because they also needed his help from time to time. Only one person was his adversary: Dr. Klein, the Latin teacher. At first he would scold Adolf for not doing his homework properly. But in the end he just ignored him, as though Adolf weren't sitting in the classroom. Adolf hated Dr. Klein, and everyone was afraid he would do something impulsive. At the end of the year, Dr. Klein refused to give him even a barely passing grade, as he had done the year before. That task fell to the assistant principal. He examined Adolf again and awarded him a low passing grade. Adolf gnashed his teeth and threatened revenge.

Adolf was different from anyone Blanca had ever known, and not only because of his height and strength. His movements were also different. Blanca was certain not only that those movements suited him, but that they were attractive in themselves. Even his way of sitting was different. Two days before her departure for the mountains, Adolf passed by her father's store, as though by chance.

"What are you doing this summer?" he asked.

"We're going to Winterweiss," she replied.

"What will you do there?"

"I'll read."

"You always read, don't you?"

"I love to read," Blanca said, blushing.

The next day they set out for Winterweiss. Her father's face took on a pleasant look. The second-class car was half empty, and the green landscapes rushed past them as they did every year.

"What are you planning to study, Blanca?" her father asked jovially.

"Mathematics," Blanca said without hesitation.

"That's just what I wanted to study, but my parents wanted me to be a merchant. I'll never forgive them."

"Not even now?"

"Papa has forgiven them," her mother interrupted.

"No, I haven't." Her father didn't give in.

On vacations, her father didn't talk about his parents or about the miserable store. Rather, he meandered among mathematics books, chess books, and literature. His suitcase was the heaviest of all, because it contained only books.

They easily found a house next to the Danube. Blanca's father was pleased, and his happiness was evident with every step he took. He swam, sunbathed, and read. Her mother prepared the foods they liked, and Blanca dreamed about Adolf. Even in her dreams she was a little frightened of him, but when she awoke, she would console herself and say, "Adolf is a sturdy person. Sturdy people are generous."

Eventually, she forgot about him. She was with her beloved

parents, and it was summer. They sat at the water's edge for hours, enjoying the long sunset, drinking lemonade, and being quiet together. Sometimes, in the evening, a peasant would stop his wagon in front of the house and offer them fish that he had just then caught in his net.

"Mama," Blanca said anxiously.

"What, dear?"

"Nothing."

The thought that she would have to part from her parents one day shocked her.

7

THAT WAS THE last summer Blanca spent with her parents, and she remembered it in full detail. During the winter her mother became ill, and the doctors promised that she would feel better in the spring. As if in spite, the winter was long, and her mother tried in vain to rise to her feet. Her father promised repeatedly, "In the spring, you'll get some relief," and it seemed to Blanca that the tone of his voice was not as it had been in the past. He spoke as though he had rehearsed what he was saying.

In high school Blanca was hugely successful. Once again, her grades glowed on her report card. Her mother took the card in her hands, and the joy that had been on her face during the summer lit it once again.

"There's an excellent mathematics department in Berlin," her father announced, as if he were capable of paying for it. The store stood on rickety foundations and barely supported the family. Her father would return home every evening and immediately sit down next to her mother. His look was full of devotion. The store and his partner depressed him to the dust, and only at his beloved wife's side did he receive some solace.

At the beginning of the next term, the assistant principal proposed that Blanca help Adolf in mathematics and Latin, and Blanca agreed. Adolf came to her house in the afternoon, and they did their homework together. The work was very difficult for him, and when he left the house his face would be red and sweaty, as after hard labor.

"How's Adolf coming along?" her mother asked.

"It's hard for him, but it seems to me that he's improving."

Sometimes her mother would address him directly.

"How are you, Adolf?" she would ask.

"Fine, thank you, ma'am," he would say, blushing.

Adolf did do his homework, but he failed the oral examination in Latin. Dr. Klein had no pity on him, and at the end of the term he gave Adolf a failing grade. Dr. Weiss, the mathematics teacher, was more generous and gave him a barely passing grade. Blanca tried to soften his disappointment, but Adolf was angry. It had always been the case, he argued, that the mathematics and Latin teachers had mistreated him. In the other subjects, he did fine. Blanca didn't correct him. She saw his shame and felt sorry for him.

"The Jewish teachers hate me," he said, chuckling.

"Dr. Klein converted in his youth," she pointed out.

"Why does he have a Jewish name, then?"

Blanca's father didn't know how to relate to Adolf.

"That boy has no human manners," he would say. "A tree will grow from a tall boy like that, not a human being."

"You mustn't talk that way," her mother scolded.

"Short people know their place in the world; the big ones always get confused."

"I refuse to listen," said her mother, blocking her ears.

That was the way her father used to joke. Sometimes he would describe people grotesquely, but he would then retract the descriptions and excuse himself. Her mother knew his little weaknesses but still didn't let him get away with it.

"Ida, you're terrible."

"Why?"

"Not even one generalization?"

"Generalizations are worse than prejudices."

"You're right. I give in."

This was one of her father's ways of teasing that Blanca liked to hear.

Spring came, and Blanca's mother felt better. Her father would take her easy chair out into the garden, wrap her in a blanket, and sit by her side. Her weakness wasn't evident in their home. The house was spotless, aired out, and filled with her gentle spirit. Blanca would return from school and tell her mother every detail about her day. Her mother would listen intently, to avoid missing anything. In the evening they would all sit and talk. But sometimes a frightening billow of sobs would burst forth from Blanca. Her mother would rush over to her and comfort her.

So the spring passed. Blanca's mother continued to feel better, and in the evening she would water the garden and take pleasure in the flowers and the lilac bushes that adorned their small yard.

"Mama," Blanca would call.

"What, dear?"

"Let me give you a kiss."

"What's the matter?"

"Nothing."

That spring Blanca was very sensitive, and every movement alarmed her.

8

EVEN BEFORE THE end of the school year, Adolf was told that he couldn't stay in high school. Dr. Klein and Dr. Weiss demanded his expulsion. The pleas of the assistant principal and some of the other teachers were to no avail. The decision to expel Adolf passed by a single vote. The announcement was sent to him in writing, and Adolf, in his fury, burned all his mathematics and Latin books in the school yard, shouting out loud, "Death to Klein! Death to Weiss! Long live freedom!"

Blanca returned from school in tears. Her pupil, whom she had tried so hard to help, had failed. Her mother tried in vain to console her.

"Klein and Weiss were cruel to him," Blanca said angrily, still weeping.

The next day Blanca met Adolf at school. His face was furious and closed. Students surrounded him and tried to cheer him up, but Adolf rejected their efforts.

"I'm not upset," he said. "The ones who failed me will pay the price."

"I'm sorry, Adolf," Blanca said, trying to take some of the blame on herself.

"You're not to blame. It's Klein and Weiss," he said drily.

Adolf's face was frightening, but Blanca didn't leave his side.

"I don't like pity," he said repeatedly. "I've declared war, and I won't be deterred." That was clear in his appearance. The skin of his face was taut, and his lips were set in a firm line—which was exactly what Blanca found so enchanting.

"Good God," she said when she got home. "Why are good people hurt? Why are they made to fail? People ought to be judged favorably, to bring out the good in them. So what if someone has trouble with mathematics or Latin? Is that a reason to expel him from school? What harm did he do?"

The school year ended, and Adolf was not among those who received report cards. His absence was conspicuous, because no boy in the school was as tall or as broad as he was. The excellent grades that sparkled on Blanca's report card didn't make her as happy as they had in the past. It seemed to her that they had come at Adolf's expense.

"In mathematics there are those who are good and those who are better," said her father enigmatically.

"Is that why they don't let students study and expel them from school?" Blanca asked.

"What can you do? That's nature."

"Isn't our motto that everyone should work according to their ability and receive according to their needs?"

"That principle doesn't apply to the study of mathematics."

"If mathematics leads to discrimination, I don't want anything more to do with it."

"Dear, you're going too far."

"I'm completely serious."

Blanca's father was proud of her, and now, hearing her opinions, he was even prouder. Her mother didn't enter the argument. In matters of logic, her husband and daughter were better than she. Every time they caught her in a contradiction, she would say, "I raise my hands in surrender."

That summer they didn't go to Winterweiss. The doctors ordered Blanca's mother to rest at home.

"I'm sorry, Blanca," her mother said.

"Why are you saying you're sorry, Mama?"

"Because of me, we're not going to Winterweiss."

"What are you talking about, Mama? I love being at home."

Meanwhile, Adolf surprised Blanca by inviting her out for a bowl of ice cream. They sat in the busy café, and Adolf told her about his plans. Next month he would start working at a dairy, and he would be making a living. He was tired of being dependent on his parents. A man should work and make money.

Blanca was embarrassed and didn't say a word. Being close to Adolf's strength dazzled her.

"And you're going to go on studying?" he asked, like someone who had himself been liberated from such things.

"What can I do?" She wanted to draw near to him.

"Aren't you tired of it?"

"In another year, I'll finish, too."

When they parted, she, too, felt disgust for the institution called high school, which tortured the weak and raised the talented up to the skies. Her fury burned against the teachers who were so good to her, Dr. Klein and Dr. Weiss; because of them, about twenty students were expelled from school every year. High school without Adolf would be barren. "By virtue of the weak, we are humane." She had heard that once from her uncle Salo, her father's brother, who was a communist, heart and soul, and had been imprisoned for a number of years. After his release, he died suddenly of a mysterious illness.

9

FROM THEN ON, Blanca would see Adolf everywhere, in her dreams and while awake. She wanted so much to see him that she walked as far as the dairy where he worked. Adolf was surprised and embarrassed by her sudden appearance. But he recovered immediately and introduced her to his fellow workers. This was the first time Blanca heard the German peasant dialect, and she didn't understand a word of it. The workers were tall and clumsy, and the odors in the dairy were pungent and stifling.

"Why did you come here?" Adolf asked.

To see you, she was about to say, but then she thought better of it and said simply, "I was taking a walk."

"Isn't there any school today?"

"There is, but I took a little vacation."

"I understand," he said, but showed no sign of excitement at her presence. But that very lack of emotion enchanted her. She interpreted it as inner quietness, as natural behavior, as masculinity of the proper kind.

Blanca's thoughts were now filled with fantasies of Adolf. *When will I see him again?* she wondered. Her grades were no longer as brilliant as they used to be.

"What's the matter with you, Blanca?" Dr. Klein wondered.

"I don't know." She didn't reveal even the slightest thing.

Dr. Weiss was more merciful and spoke to her like a father. "Blanca," he said, "you have all the talent and potential of a mathematician. Please, do yourself a favor, concentrate, and make an effort so we can give you a scholarship to study in Vienna. The mathematics department in Berlin may be better, but they're no slouches in Vienna, either. I don't have many students like you."

"I'll try," she said to mollify him.

"For the sake of your future, my dear."

Blanca didn't want to reveal her deepest thoughts to them. Ever since Adolf had been expelled, she hated the high school, and the mathematics and Latin classes in particular. It seemed to her that the continued existence of that arrogant institution was for nothing but the persecution of Adolf's soul. She remembered how Adolf had carried desks on his broad shoulders from classroom to classroom, and she felt a stabbing in her heart. That was the gratitude they showed him. Anyone who lacked an analytical brain was banished to the dairy.

"I won't lend a hand to it," she said to her father one evening, but her father was so preoccupied with the business of his store that he didn't notice her anger. "That's right," he replied distractedly.

Blanca used to meet Adolf from time to time in the street or near the tavern. He was well liked everywhere, and people gathered around him. Sometimes she would pass him without his noticing her. One evening, on her way home, he approached her and said, "What are you doing here?"

"I'm on my way home."

"How'd you like to have a beer?"

"Gladly."

Blanca had never been in a tavern, although she had read a lot about them. Dim lights illuminated the corners of the room, the gramophone blared, and the smells of beer and smoke billowed up to the ceiling. On a low stage couples danced, kissed, and cuddled.

"Do you plan to study at the university?"

"I haven't decided yet."

"All the young Jews are sent to the university, right?"

First, not all the young Jews, she was about to say, *and, second, they aren't sent. People have free will and the ability to choose, and they go of their own accord, not because they're sent.* But she controlled herself and said simply, "I don't know."

Adolf didn't realize that her answer was evasive.

"All the young Jews are sent to the university," he insisted. "I know."

"What's wrong with that?" she asked.

"I don't know what's wrong with it, but it certainly isn't good."

Logic wasn't Adolf's strong suit, and whenever he got stuck, he became obstinate. But Blanca found charm in that stammering as well, and, rather than criticizing his response, she was enchanted, as if she had been shown a wild spot where rare flowers grew.

"I met Adolf," she told her mother. "He's working in a dairy."

"Poor fellow."

"I prefer the dairy to high school. In the dairy there's no distinction between one person and another. There people aren't tested on their knowledge of mathematics and Latin every week."

"You're right, dear." Her mother knew in her heart that Blanca's argument was flawed, but once her daughter had entered high school, she no longer commented on anything she said. She would say to herself that a girl who excels in mathematics and Latin, who is admired by her teachers, and who is a candidate for the prestigious Salzburg Prize certainly knows what she's talking about. That was also how she felt about her husband. She was certain that one day his talents would come to light, and he would even do wonders in business.

While Blanca was wondering in her heart where to go and what to do, Adolf came and made the decision for her. He did it the way he did everything, directly and bluntly.

It was in the evening, and they were sitting in the tavern and joking about how short Klein was, how he saw the world through a dwarf's eyes. Blanca was the one who raised the idea of dwarfs,

and Adolf, because of his hatred for Klein, added a few humor-
ous outlines. Now it seemed that a strong emotion bound them
together: Klein's dwarflike appearance and the hatred he aroused
in both of them.

For a long while they laughed, and Blanca was pleased that she
had managed to make a mockery of the man who had expelled
Adolf from high school. As Adolf was walking her home and they
were laughing about Klein and Weiss, he said to her, almost casually, "How would you like to be my wife?"

"Me?" Blanca said.

"You."

"You're joking."

"I don't joke about such things."

"It's only that it's a surprise for me."

"I'm a Christian, and Christians don't joke about such things."

It was a simple trap, and she was caught in it. Later she would say
to herself, *How was I trapped? How did I fail to see? What blinded me
so? After all, I was a person who stood on her own two feet, someone
with an awareness of the world.* But that evening she was drunk
with happiness, so drunk that she didn't dare tell her secret even
to her beloved mother. It was not until the next morning that she
revealed her engagement to her mother, who caught her breath,
hugged Blanca, and burst into tears.

10

BLANCA WANTED TO TELL Otto everything, to describe in detail
the insults she had borne over the years, what she had done to herself and to others, and how blind she had been. It was important
to her now for no detail to get lost, so that when the time came,
Otto would know the course of events in full. Every night she sat
down and wrote. First she was particular about the order of events,
but time made a fool of her, and everything got mixed up together.
No matter, she said to herself, *Otto will understand by himself what
came first and what came afterward. The main thing is that no detail
should be unknown to him.*

Sometimes a bad dream would disturb Otto's sleep, and he
would awaken in a panic.

"It's nothing, dear, dreams speak hollow words." She hugged
him tightly.

"I dreamed about Papa," he told her.

"And what happened?"

"It was very frightening."

"There's nothing to be afraid of, dear. Would you like something hot?"

"What are you doing, Mama?"

"I'm writing."

"What are you writing?"

"Memories."

"What are memories?"

"Everything that was and will never be again."

"I'll write someday, too."

"Certainly."

Otto grew and changed. The memory of the house was gradually erased from his mind, and he sank into daydreams and into his games. Blanca didn't interfere. The thought that time was short, and that she had to leave Otto a detailed account, drove her to the writing table night after night. But the order of their days remained unaffected. Until sunset they would tarry by the water, and in the evening they would go out for a walk along the riverbank. After the walk, Otto would sink down on the mat and fall asleep, and Blanca would fall upon her notebook and write until after midnight.

Sometimes an image from distant childhood would intrude, and it was crystal clear. At first she would ignore it, saying to herself, *I have to be faithful to order, to write only what touches upon this affair.* In time she ceased that, realizing that distant memories also belonged in her account. Memories of Grandpa and Grandma and her uncle Salo.

She concluded a long chapter with the words "I did what I did, and I am prepared to submit to justice for it."

11

IT WAS FIVE MONTHS after her marriage, and Blanca, in the city where she was born, had no one close to her. Everyone appeared to have conspired to ignore her. Grandma Carole stood at the entrance to the synagogue every day and cursed the converts. Her closed face, withered from the sun, was now even more threatening. Blanca would make her purchases in the market hurriedly and then escape. Adolf would return from the dairy late, irritable, demanding his meal right away. If the meal didn't suit him, he would say, "It's tasteless. You have to learn how to cook a meal."

After he slapped her face, she seldom left the house, taking care only to purchase what was needed and to heat the bathwater. Every week a postcard came from the mountains, reminding her that she had a father and a sick mother. In the morning, when she was alone, she would remember that less than a year ago, she was studying in high school. She had been an outstanding student, and her parents were proud of her. Now it all seemed so distant, as if it had never happened. In the afternoon, fear would possess her, and she wouldn't leave her room. Her hands trembled, and every movement cost her great effort.

More than once she said to herself, *I mustn't be afraid. Fear is humiliating, and one must overcome it.* But it didn't help. Ever since Adolf had slapped her, she was afraid of every shadow and wanted only to do his will, like a maidservant. Strangely, just at those moments of dread, she remembered Grandma Carole. *If a blind old woman can stand in front of the synagogue and curse and not be afraid,* she said to herself, *I, too, mustn't fear.*

Once, she mustered courage and said to Adolf, "I'm afraid."

"What are you afraid of?" he said with a coldness that sent chills down her spine.

"I don't know."

"Jews are always afraid. A Christian woman doesn't fear."

Once a week, usually on Sunday, Adolf's parents would visit. They were tall and broad, and their faces reflected a strange mixture of piety, obtuseness, and anger. Their clothes reeked of alcohol. At their side, Adolf was obedient and submissive.

"Yes, I didn't think of that," he would say.

The three of them together would suck all the air out of the living room.

Once Adolf's mother said to her, "Blanca, you have to change your name. That name isn't common among us."

Blanca was frightened. "That's true," she said.

"You don't have to choose. The priest will pick a name for you."

Blanca rushed to the kitchen to bring out some sauerkraut, and the conversation went elsewhere. Meanwhile, Blanca's parents had come back from the mountains. Her mother had made up her mind to die in her own bed and not in a strange place. Her father ignored the doctors' advice and submitted to his wife's wishes.

"Forgive me," Blanca's mother said to her astonished daughter. "My days in this world will not be many. I won't disturb you too much."

A doctor came one morning and examined her, gave her an injection of morphine, and left no doubt in the hearts of those who loved her that her illness was mortal, that they must prepare for the inevitable.

"What can I do?" asked her father in a broken voice.

"Nothing," said the doctor.

But the next day a miracle happened. Blanca's mother rose from her bed and sat down at the table. Her father, stunned, looked at her as if she had lost her mind.

"Why did you get out of bed?" he asked.

"I feel better."

"The doctor said that you mustn't get out of bed," he murmured with a trembling voice.

When he realized that she did indeed feel better, he made her a cup of tea and sat by her side.

"What happened?" he asked.

"I saw my sister Tina in a dream, the way I haven't seen her for years, and she told me to get out of bed. I didn't believe I could, and I said to her, 'Excuse me, Tina, I'm ill.' 'Now you're not ill,' Tina said to me."

"And what happened after that?"

"She sat by my side the way you're sitting by my side."

"And what else did she say to you?"

"I don't remember."

When Blanca saw her mother sitting at the table, she went down on her knees.

"Mother, what am I seeing?" she said.

Blanca was glad that her parents had come back, but to tell them what had happened to her, how she was enslaved—she didn't dare.

She sat at her mother's bedside without saying a word. Her mother saw, with a feeling of helplessness, that Blanca's way of moving had changed. She was thinner. Her eyes were puffy, and her lips formed a thin, tight line. It was hard for her to talk, because it was hard for her to say what was oppressing her.

Blanca's father was entangled in debts. His elder brother, Theodor, did send them a small sum from Hungary every month, but it wasn't enough. In vain he sought other sources of income. Finally, he sold some of his wife's jewels.

Blanca's mother parted from her jewels with a heavy heart. "I intended to give them to Blanca," she said.

"Mama," said Blanca, "I don't need jewels."

"I'm just a guest here for the moment, dear. These hours were given to me as a gift."

"What gift are you talking about, Mama?"

"These hours, dear."

The house seemed to change in appearance. Blanca's mother's breathing was weak, and the shadows cast by her arms were longer than her arms themselves, but her eyes were wide open. Blanca momentarily forgot the misery of life in her own home. The light of her mother's life surrounded her with a circle of warmth, and words like none she had ever heard, words like the sounds of prayer, trembled on her lips.

12

TWO MONTHS AFTER her return from the mountains, in mid-July, Blanca's mother passed away.

"Ida, what has happened to you?" her stunned father cried out.

"Ida will suffer no longer," said the doctor, in the solemn tones of a priest.

"And what can I do?" her father asked in a subdued voice.

"There's nothing more to be done," answered the doctor, sounding pleased that he had an occasion to say that. Blanca's father ran to Blanca's house.

Adolf noticed him coming.

"Your father's running like a madman."

"Who's running?" Blanca didn't catch what he said.

"I already told you."

"Blanca!" her father called out, and stumbled.

Toward evening a quorum of ten Jewish men came from Himmelburg with a woman to wash the body in ritual preparation for burial and to say prayers. Grandma Carole, who deafened the city with her shouts, now stood as silent as a mountain. The burial society organized the funeral. Its head, a tall, dignified man, sat next to Blanca's father as though he were his elder brother and spoke to him in a somber manner. Blanca's father did not weep. But his unshaven face and swollen eyes displayed rigid shock.

"When will the funeral begin?" he roused himself to ask.

"Soon," said the man.

"And who will say kaddish?"

"You will, sir."

"Not I!" Blanca's father said in anguish. "I don't know it. I've forgotten it."

"I'll say it in your place," said the man.

Hearing his answer, her father hung his head, as though relieved.

Not many people came to the cemetery. Three of Ida's friends came, high school classmates, two neighbors who had converted, and a few people who had known Blanca's father in his youth. Blanca's father grasped the arm of the head of the burial society.

"I forgot the kaddish," he murmured. "I don't remember anything of it."

"Not to worry, I'll say it," the stranger promised him again.

"I thank you from the depths of my heart," Blanca's father mumbled.

Blanca did not approach Grandma Carole. She was afraid her grandmother would slap her. But to everyone's surprise, her grandmother didn't grumble, question anything, or interfere. When they lowered the casket into the grave, Blanca hugged her father and sank her face into his chest.

After the service, Grandma Carole rushed away, heading for the open field. Everyone stood still for a moment and watched her go. A few yards away lay the Christian cemetery. Its tall marble monuments gleamed in the sunlight, making the unmistakable point that sometimes death has a finer dwelling than a Jewish graveyard.

Blanca's father, who had been holding on to the arm of the head of the burial society, finally let it go.

"Ladies and gentlemen," he called out clearly, "we mustn't scatter and leave Ida alone here." He meant to add something but, seeing that everyone had stopped walking and was standing in amazement, he fell silent.

"I will stay here," he added a moment later. "I'm not afraid."

"Papa," Blanca called out, "I won't let you stay here alone."

The head of the burial society approached him, hugged him in front of everyone, and said, "We Jews stand by one another."

The word "Jews," as it left the tall man's mouth, startled those in attendance with its simple clarity. Most of them were converts. "Ida couldn't bear it any longer," Blanca's father said, removing his hat.

The tall man, whose heart was touched by Blanca's father's distress, said, "You mustn't fear. Death redeemed her from her sufferings, and we must accept the judgment."

"True," said her father, although he was put off by the man's confident tone.

"Life after death is a life with no suffering. All our sources speak of that explicitly and simply."

"I didn't know," said her father in the voice of a man who has been beaten.

"There is no reason to worry," the man said in a different tone of voice. "The condition of the Jews in this region isn't splendid, but we stand by one another. We shall support you. We won't let you fall."

13

DURING THE SEVEN-DAY mourning period, Blanca's father sat in the living room with a skullcap on his head, distractedly receiving the few visitors. That quiet man, who had said little over the years, now spoke at length, mainly about his late wife, whose many talents were never properly expressed. He spoke about her musical ear, about her talent for writing, and he showed the visitors the landscapes in the living room, which she had painted when she was in high school. Blanca sat with him all morning, prepared his meals, and at noon she returned to her home. The hours in the company of her grieving father brought her surprising consolation. More than once she was on the verge of telling him about the harsh insults that were her lot at home, but seeing that he was completely immersed in his grief, she didn't dare. Mourning cut off his ordinary life, a life of sorrow and worry about the coming day, and brought him to a world that was all mercy. Blanca, having no alternative, was forced to take care of all the practical matters: preparing to sell the house, paying his debts. Blanca's father didn't realize what distress his daughter was in, and he would say, "You're still young, and your life lies before you."

Adolf would return late at night and whip her with his belt. Now he didn't hit her in anger, but with the intention of hurting her. "We have to uproot all your weaknesses from you and all the bad qualities you inherited from your parents. A woman has to be a woman and not a weakling." In bed he behaved like an animal, turning her over like a mattress, and afterward he would get out of bed, drink some brandy, and say, "What kind of woman are you? You don't know how to be a woman."

"What should I do?" she asked, trembling. All her efforts to please Adolf were in vain. He hit her and cursed her.

"What do you want from me?"

"To be a woman and not a Jewess."

"I'm not a Jewess anymore."

"One baptism's not enough, apparently."

She would cry, and her weeping drove him crazy. He would throw a tantrum and curse her and her ancestors, who didn't know how to live right, bound up with money and flawed in character.

On Sundays his brothers and friends would fill the house; they would guzzle and gobble and finally sing and dance in the yard until late at night. The next day she would get up early to make Adolf his morning coffee. After he left the house, dizziness would assail her, and she would sink to the floor, ravaged.

When she could no longer keep it all in, she told something of it to her father.

"Everything isn't going so well at home."

"Why not?" her father asked, with a kind of obtuse surprise.

"Adolf isn't the way he was."

"Everything will work out. You mustn't worry," her father replied superficially.

Blanca's father's debts proved to be many. The head of the Himmelburg burial society did keep his promise, and every week he brought some food and a bit of money, but where would her father live after the house was sold? That was now Blanca's concern. True, there was an old age home in nearby Himmelburg, but it was small and fully occupied, and old people were on a waiting list to be accepted there.

Her father didn't seem concerned. Day after day he was inundated with fantasies, and they bore him from place to place. Once, he said, "I have to get to Vienna and try to get a scholarship. All the grades in my matriculation certificate were excellent."

"And what will you study?"

"What do you mean? Mathematics!"

Hearing those words, Blanca would freeze. Now she was no longer in doubt: her father had departed along with her mother, and what remained of him was just embers. More and more he talked about his high school days, when he had studied with Ida. He had been regarded as a genius, and everyone expected great things of him. More and more he blamed his parents for not helping him study in Vienna. He even mentioned Grandma Carole several times, always with harsh anger. Ida was the only one of whom he spoke gently, as though she were still with him.

But there were also moments of clarity. The clouds of fantasy in which he had entrenched himself would disperse, and he saw what he didn't want to see: his misery. Then he would suddenly say, "Blanca, I'm hopeless. I have to get out of here as soon as possible. I don't want to be a burden."

"Why are you hurting me, Papa?"

These, of course, were merely flashes. The clouds would surround him once more, and his face would darken or suddenly change and become awkwardly merry. Adolf's opinion was uncompromising. "We have to bring him to the old age home in Himmelburg and give the institution no alternative. Don't worry, they won't dare contradict me."

She tried to stop him. "Not yet," she said.

"You're too preoccupied with him," he declared.

The next day they went. Her father didn't object. A simple, awkward smile sat on his face, as though he knew that he would not escape from Adolf's grasp. The train trip took about an hour, and they reached the old age home before lunch. The manager, not a young woman, explained to them that the place was full beyond capacity and that even the corridors were taken. Adolf was determined to leave her father there, no matter what.

The elderly manager listened and repeated her arguments. She showed him the corridor, crammed with beds. "There's no room, good people," she said, spreading her arms.

"If there are twenty beds, one can be added," Adolf argued with force.

In the end, when she proved to him how wrong he was, Adolf didn't restrain himself. He pounded on the table and said, "The Jews have to take him in. If they don't take him in, this building will go up in flames. You can't talk to Jews in any other language."

The manager turned pale, asked for consideration, and finally raised her hands and said, "What can I do?"

Thus was Blanca's father abandoned. He stood there, stunned. Then he hugged Blanca and said, "Go home, child. Everything is all right." Blanca promised to bring him more clothing and his shaving kit.

"Don't forget to bring the chess set."

Adolf rushed Blanca out. Her father suddenly raised his right hand and called out loud, "Be well, children, and take care of yourselves."

14

RIGHT AFTER THAT, Blanca sold the house and paid the debts, and there was some cash left over to give to her father. She was glad she managed to finish that matter. She left for Himmelburg on the morning train to tell her father about the sale. She found him sitting in bed, wearing striped pajamas. A strange merriness glowed in his eyes. Hearing her words, he said, "How is Mama? Do we have to bring her to a rest home again?"

"No."

"Thank God."

Then, with no transition, he asked her to bring him his mathematics books because he wanted to freshen his knowledge. About the place itself he said nothing.

It was her father, but he was not really himself. His cheeks were red, and a kind of childish astonishment lit up his face. The things that perturbed him at home still perturbed him here, but now he added, "No matter."

"How is Grandma Carole?"

"She's quite fine," Blanca answered.

"She's always fine," her father said mischievously.

The director told her the absolute truth. He wasn't living in reality, and he had to be treated like a child. The old age home couldn't bear the expense of taking care of him.

Hearing her words, Blanca buried her face in her hands and burst into tears.

"What can I do?" she cried. "I have nothing of my own, and my husband won't let me work outside of the house."

The elderly director, seeing her youth and distress, exerted no more pressure on her.

"Don't abandon your father," she said. "Come to visit him often."

"Of course I'll come. I have no one else in the world beside him."

The director also told Blanca that most of the residents were abandoned. The children had converted to Christianity and denied their old parents. The financial condition of the institution was precarious, and were it not for bequests from some of those who died, the place would have been closed long ago. Blanca promised to come and help, and the elderly director hugged her, saying, "You're a loyal daughter, and the Jewish spark is not extinguished in your heart."

"That's my grip on this world, believe me," Blanca said with emotion.

"There are so few of us, and we are worn so thin," said the director, and it was clear that the burden on her shoulders was too heavy to bear.

From then on, Blanca's days were oppressive and disheartening.

"Let me see Papa," Blanca would beg. "I'll come back in the afternoon." But Adolf refused.

"You have to cut yourself off from them."

"But he's my father."

"I said what I said."

It was power and dread bound up together. Blanca was so weak that everything Adolf said or did seemed correct to her. At night she would wake up and ask, "Where am I?" She was gradually disintegrating.

Again help came to her from heaven. Adolf went off for a week of occupational training in the Tyrolean Mountains, and Blanca rushed out that very morning. This time, too, she found her father sitting on the bed. His face had grown thin, and a strange spirituality glowed in it.

At first he didn't recognize her. But then he did, and called out, "Look, it's my Blanca. It's my daughter." Not a minute passed before he rose from his bed and asked, "How's Mama? How does she feel?"

"Fine," Blanca replied.

"And we won't have to take her to a rest home?"

"No."

"Thank God."

Then it was as if all his words had faded away. Blanca didn't know what to say, either, so she was silent. The man lying next to him asked, "Who's that pretty girl?"

"My daughter, Blanca."

"She looks a lot like you."

"She's my only daughter, and I have no other children."

"I have three sons, but they don't come to visit me."

"Where do they live?"

"Not far from here."

Blanca hadn't forgotten about her father's request. She brought a package of mathematics books. Although the books had turned yellow with the years, they excited her father.

"I'll start right away," he said in his former tone of voice.

Blanca gathered the clothes that were stuffed into the cupboard and went out to wash them. The laundry, a broad, half-dark room with green stains on its walls, gave off a heavy odor of dampness and mildew. The sink, the washboard, and the water in the tubs evoked images of her childhood and of Johanna, their cleaning woman, who had left the house about two years before her mother's death because her father could no longer pay her. She was a devout Christian, and her long, narrow room was full of sacred images and the fragrance of incense. While Blanca was still a child, Johanna used to place her on her knees, remove the image of Jesus from the wall, and say, "This is Jesus. He is the savior of the world, and we pray to him morning and night." This made a great impression on Blanca, and she kept that secret in her heart, without revealing a hint of it to her parents.

When Blanca was in high school, already full of knowledge, excelling in the exact sciences, enthusiastic about Rousseau and Marx, and positive that religion would ultimately disappear from the world, she continued to visit Johanna in her room and talk to her. Once Johanna told her, in the tones of a person firm in her faith, "Whoever refuses to acknowledge our Redeemer will not be saved."

Blanca wanted to laugh. But seeing the devotion in Johanna's face, she controlled herself and asked, "And the Jews won't be saved?"

"No, to my regret."

"Why not, Johanna?"

"Because they refuse to accept His mercy."

Back then Johanna's beliefs had sounded old-fashioned and unfounded. Blanca was confident that those superstitions would ultimately fade away, and that the doctrines of Rousseau and Marx would fill everyone's heart.

Before an hour had gone by, Blanca had washed everything, and then went out to hang the laundry on the clotheslines. Contact with those familiar shirts, which Johanna and, later, Blanca's mother used to wash on the rear balcony, reminded her of her mother's slow, tormented death. A few days before she died, Blanca's mother had said to Blanca, "Take care of Papa. Life hasn't been kind to him."

"Mama, why are you worried?" Blanca had said.

When she returned to the corridor, she found her father immersed in the effort to solve a mathematical problem. He was on his knees next to a small trunk, with the books scattered on his bed. For Blanca this was a sight from earlier times, when she herself had studied mathematics.

"Papa," she said as she approached him.

"What's the matter, dear?" He raised his face to her.

"Are the problems hard?"

"Not especially."

"I have to go home, Papa."

"Go in peace, dear," he said distractedly.

"I'll come back soon," she said, and kissed his forehead.

"Very good," he replied, and sank into his notebook.

.

It was very painful to Blanca that her good father, whom she wanted to sit next to and tell about all the humiliations and fears that had been her lot during the past months, that her good, sensitive father had departed from the world. What remained of him was a high school boy, all of whose grades were excellent. Now the boy was burrowing into mathematics books to show everyone that he was better than Lutzky and Levi, the two Jewish boys in his class who were his competitors. Lutzky and Levi had become industrialists. They had conquered the Austrian market and expanded across the provinces as far as distant Bukovina. And he had remained stuck in his stationery store with his cousin Dachs.

15

WHEN SHE RETURNED HOME in the early afternoon, Blanca realized that her life was now merely a smoldering ember. Overcome with fear, she went to the sink and washed the dishes. Then she began to chop the vegetables and dice the meat the way Adolf had told her to.

While she was cutting and preparing, Blanca remembered that Adolf wasn't coming back that night. Six full days still lay at her disposal. She cautiously stepped over to the armchair and sank into it. For a long time she sat, withdrawn into herself. Only after the sun began to set, so that its light fell upon the wall opposite her, did a feeling of ease, such as she had not felt for a long while, spread down her back and arms.

Later, she changed her clothes and went outdoors. The afternoon light was full, but chilly and colorless. At this time of the year, the examinations in school were at their most intense. Blanca would study hard, delving into complicated subjects and resolving mathematical problems. The examinations required an exhausting effort, but victory was not slow in coming.

"I have one 'Excellent,' " Dr. Weiss would announce, and everyone knew whom he was talking about. There was a Jewish boy named Theo Braunstein in her class, a student of average ability who tried to claim a piece of the crown for himself. He was self-important, squinty-eyed, and ridiculous in his ambition. Everybody knew that no one was better than Blanca at solving complicated problems. Theo tried to woo her by showing off his mathematical prowess. Everybody knew that two private tutors were helping him and equipping him with all sorts of unusual examples to make an impression on the teachers. He didn't impress Blanca. Blanca didn't like the way he made a show of his knowledge, flattered the teachers, and acted insulted when a grade didn't suit him. She rejected his attentions.

Now he is probably studying at the university, she thought. *Soon he'll be a doctor or a lawyer.* Strange, but that passing thought imperceptibly restored something of herself. She was pleased that she had those memories. Once she had been an admired student; anyone who couldn't solve a mathematics problem would turn to her, and she would solve it. It occurred to her that it would be nice to visit one of her friends, the way she used to do not many years ago. But then she realized that she had no close friends; the few that she once had were married or had gone off to other cities. There had been one good friend, Anna, a tall, attractive girl, with whom she liked to converse. They used to talk about school—about the teachers and, of course, about the other students. Anna had insights that made Blanca laugh: she noticed the way the students dressed, how they sat, and how they raised their hands. Blanca, on the other hand, was immersed in her books. They were her whole world, and if she wanted conversation, she talked with her parents. She didn't know how to observe people. In the last two years of high school, a great change took place in Anna's behavior. The pretty, open girl gradually closed up. She spoke little and hardly took part in class-room discussions. She grew thin, and her face became shriveled. One day she told Blanca that she had decided to enter the church and follow a religious way of life.

Blanca was stunned. "Do you pray every day?"

"Yes."

"What happened to you?" Blanca asked, and immediately regretted the question.

None of the Jewish girls Blanca knew well was devoted to her faith. Nor were the Jewish converts to Christianity. But among the

Christian girls, there were some who spoke about the convent as a possibility for their lives. Anna confided in her: only a religious life was meaningful. Any other life was insipid and miserable. At the time, Anna's words had seemed like a narrowness of mind to Blanca. Blanca saw the world in the form of mathematical and chemical formulas and, sometimes, through the struggle to change society.

"I don't want to be like my parents," Anna told her.

"Why?"

"There's a kind of weary insipidity to their lives."

The expression "weary insipidity," which Anna pronounced sharply, revealed the change that had taken place in her. She was no longer that lighthearted Anna who observed people and noticed their weaknesses. Now she was a different Anna—inhibited, and with a few deep lines of sorrow already creasing her face. Blanca kept her distance from her. From time to time they met, but their conversations weren't as they had been in the past. Blanca was certain that Anna had been captured by a useless faith, and that she would regret it.

The grocer told Blanca that Anna was now a nun and that she had been living for several years in a convent in the Mensen Mountains. Once a year, right after Christmas, she would come down from the convent and visit her parents.

"How far is it to there?"

"There's no regular transportation. You go up from the railway station by foot."

When she went back out into the street, Blanca saw Grandma Carole standing in front of the synagogue's locked doors. Her blind face was taut and her eyelids quivered. Passersby looked at her with contempt and called her names, but she stood at attention in her place and didn't react. *That old blind woman, my mother's mother, is now standing alone against the mob, receiving insults but not leaving her post,* Blanca thought. That thought erased the feelings of estrangement that had for years dwelled in her heart, and Blanca looked upon Grandma Carole not as her prickly grandmother but as a brave woman who was fighting for her principles.

While Blanca was observing her, the blind woman began to cry. From her shattered syllables, it was hard at first for Blanca to understand why she was crying. But then Blanca recognized names that she knew, among them the daughter who had died too young and Grandma Carole's three grandchildren, who had become apostates. It wasn't the weeping of someone who was disoriented, but of a mourner. Passersby, as well as the nearby shopkeepers who had gotten used to her shouting and curses over time, stood in amazement. No one approached her. Her sightless eyes continued to roll, and her weeping became swallowed up inside her.

Eventually she stretched out her cane and turned right, in the direction of her house. Blanca wanted to follow her and accompany her home, but she didn't dare. Instead, she went into the nearby tavern and drank two glasses of cognac. The burning liquid seeped into her and its warmth spread throughout her body.

In her parents' home, they didn't drink. Blanca had her first drinks under Adolf's direction. Adolf had known how to drink from his youth. At first drinking disgusted her and made her dizzy, but in time she found that two or three drinks drew her out of her despondency. Later on, after Otto's birth, Blanca fell into a deep depression, and cognac was what saved her. Now, too, cognac brought her relief. She rose and went outside, certain, for some reason, that her broken life was no longer going to be held captive. Now she had to stride forward, which is what she did. She proceeded in the direction of her house, imagining the bed upon which she would soon lay her heavy head.

16

OTTO AWOKE IN the middle of the night.

"What are you doing, Mama?" he asked.

"I'm writing."

"What are you writing?"

"My memoirs."

For a moment he was perplexed, as though he realized he had already asked that question and had been answered.

Over the past week they had spent many hours together. The days grew longer, and now the twilight lasted until midnight. Otto was awake for a long time, and Blanca didn't start writing until he collapsed on the mat. At first the sentences flowed, but now she found it hard to write a complete sentence. Fatigue and fear of coming events blocked the flow, and her sentences were fragmentary and scattered. To correct the flaws, she rewrote again and again.

Otto did not make things easier for her. He demanded attention and kept bringing up memories he had of their house. These few memories were not without meaning for him, but he knew that his mother didn't like it when he asked about the toys they had left behind. While he seldom asked questions, when they passed by the chapel and he saw the image of the crucified Christ, he didn't hold back. "Why did the Jews crucify Jesus?" he asked.

"Didn't I tell you that the Jews didn't crucify Jesus?" she replied impatiently.

"So who did crucify him?"

"The Romans."

"I didn't know."

"So get that fact into your head. The Romans crucified Jesus and not the Jews."

The years Blanca had spent with Adolf left more than physical scars on her. When she got angry, she noticed, she imitated his voice. More than once she had sworn to herself that she would uproot that violent voice from her throat, but, as though in spite, every time she got angry, it returned.

"When are we going?" Otto suddenly asked before falling asleep.

"Why are you asking, dear?"

"It looked to me like we were about to leave."

"Perhaps. Do you want to?"

"Where will we go?"

"I guess we'll go farther north."

Otto was sensitive to every movement. Two days earlier, two men who were looking for a woman named Anna Tramweill aroused Blanca's suspicion. They went from house to house, and finally they stood in the street and questioned passersby. They looked like two peasants who were searching for a debtor or a witness in a trial. In any case, she didn't like the looks of the men, and she said to Otto, "Maybe we'll have to leave soon." He usually reacted to her fears belatedly.

The landlady was very friendly to them. She told Blanca scraps of her life and praised her daughter. Her daughter not only lengthened her mother's days, but she also broadened her world. God had mercy on all His creatures, and upon her He showed particular mercy. Blanca didn't usually like that way of speaking, but from the old woman's mouth it sounded truthful.

That morning the landlady brought them a loaf of bread she had just baked, and a jar of prune jam.

"I'm sorry," Blanca said. "We might have to leave soon."

"Why so fast?"

"What can I do?" Blanca said, without going into detail.

Since encountering the two men in the street, Blanca hadn't felt tranquil. She locked the door and didn't walk as far as before. When the sun set, which was very late now, they walked up from the riverbank and Blanca made dinner. First Otto observed her handiwork, then he sat with his toys.

The day before he had asked, "When are we going to see a soccer game?"

Otto used to go to the soccer field with Adolf. After the game, Adolf would take him to his friends in the tavern. When they returned home, Otto's face would be red from the sun, and his movements would be wild. When he shouted, Adolf would slap his face the way he slapped Blanca's face, with no warning.

"A boy must behave properly. He must listen, and not get fresh," he would say. Every time a slap landed on Otto's face, Blanca would cringe, but she never said anything to Adolf. She would hug Otto and kiss the place where he was hurt, and for that she was scolded, of course.

Meanwhile, Blanca's writings piled up on the wooden table. She hadn't written since the end of high school, and the letters had become alien to her. She tried to stick to some order and to the facts, and of course to block the anger that sometimes welled up in her. She repeatedly told herself that the facts came before anything else. Without facts, there could be no reliable testimony.

17

TWO DAYS WITHOUT Adolf, and Blanca's body began to thaw out a little. Though her movements were still constricted, she was no longer afraid to go into town. A week earlier, in great despair, she had put on her mother's wristwatch. For a whole day she felt the burning touch of the strap. Now she felt that the watch was protecting her.

Blanca rose early the next morning and rushed to catch the train to Himmelburg. She had packed a bag full of vegetables and fruit, and a cheesecake she bought in a bakery, and she knew that as soon as he walked through the door Adolf would ask her about the extra expenses. But the full bag made her so happy that Adolf's return didn't concern her at all. She walked to the railway station energetically and with a self-esteem she had forgotten she had. Within a few minutes she was there.

The train arrived on time, and Blanca found a comfortable seat next to a window. Since Adolf had left the house, some visions of her distant childhood had returned to her. When her mother had taken her to school for the first time, and she had seen how rowdy the school yard was, Blanca had heard her mother say to herself, *Good God, what will my daughter do in this mob? She'll be lost.* Then, when the principal, with her sturdy appearance, called Blanca's name and told her to part from her mother and go into the classroom, her mother had taken her with both hands and said, "May God watch over you, my good little girl!" Thus, with trembling hands, she had let go of her mother. Now Blanca clearly remembered the long, high-ceilinged corridor through which she had walked every day. She also saw the frightening principal, whom she hadn't seen for years.

Blanca went to the buffet car and had two drinks, one right after the other. The thought that in less than an hour she would be with her beloved father filled her with happiness. For a moment it seemed to her that she wasn't going to the old age home in Himmelburg but to their enchanted vacation home in the Winterweiss Mountains, where they had imbibed the pleasures of the summer, reading or just sitting in silence. If there was a piano, Blanca's mother would play Mozart sonatas. In the mountains, what was hidden inside each of them—a desire to withdraw from the noisy world, a yearning for solitude—found expression. They would walk through the valleys, far from the main roads, immersed in silence.

Blanca found her father in a good mood. He told her at length, and not without humor, about the routines of the place and the ridiculous arrangements, but his cheerful behavior, which reminded her of better times and other places, filled her with sudden melancholy. She understood then that her father didn't grasp what fate had ordained for him, and where he had ended up. He was sitting on his bed in his old striped pajamas, his big impish eyes wide open. The sight of her father in his new incarnation brought a catch to her throat, and she had to stifle her tears.

When she showed him what she had brought, he kissed her forehead and said, "I have one daughter and Blanca is her name, and she is better to me than two brothers." It was no coincidence that he said "two brothers." He really did have two brothers in South America; they had sailed there when they were young. At first they had sent postcards. Then they disappeared, and not a word was heard from them.

Then Blanca's father introduced her to the people lying alongside him in the corridor. In his short stay, he had become acquainted with them. The smell of mold and burned food hung in the air. The people lying in their beds raised themselves slightly in honor of the guest. They asked about the weather and about the arrival and departure of trains, and they complained about their sons and daughters, who had not come to visit them in months.

"Your papa is a young man. What is he doing in this stable?" one of the old men asked her.

"I'm not so young, sir. I'm fifty-three already," her father answered.

"You're a child, sir. Entry here is restricted to people over seventy. People live here for a year or two and die off."

"Isn't my presence welcome?" her father asked mischievously.

"Most welcome, and very pleasant. But you mustn't be in this stable. The old horses are brought to this stable so that no one will see the torments of their demise."

"Silence!" an old man called out from a corner of the corridor.

"I'm just telling him the truth. I'm neither adding nor detracting."

"Why don't we go out and take a little walk?" Blanca was surprised to find that her voice had returned to her.

"What for, dear?"

"To see Himmelburg, an ancient and beautiful city."

"I don't feel like getting dressed."

"Not even in honor of me?"

That sentence did what only a magic word can do. Her father put on his fine winter suit, he placed his hat on his head, and they left the corridor as though they were visitors. Her father, she found, was familiar with Himmelburg from past years. At one time he had wanted to buy a bookstore there, and the deal almost went through, but Grandma Carole had interfered. She claimed that the store wasn't profitable and that he would do better to buy a store in Heimland, where people knew one another.

For a moment it seemed to Blanca that her father had returned to his old self and in a little while he would come home. But then she remembered that the house had been sold, and if Adolf knew that he had slept in their house, he would beat her.

"Papa," she said.

"What, dear?"

"Himmelburg is a very pretty city, prettier than Heimland."

"In my youth I used to come here often."

"What for, Papa?"

"I had a girlfriend here."

"And what happened?"

"I liked your mother better."

They sat in a café, and Blanca's father told her that although he had all the qualifications to be accepted as a student in the mathematics department at the university in Vienna, his parents, who had the means to support him, wouldn't let him go. Blanca knew very well how things had turned out. But this time her father added new details, and it was clear that he had never forgiven his parents for that injustice. And that was also why he had distanced himself from everything Jewish. Blanca's father spoke in an orderly, logical way. He mentioned his partner Dachs and Grandma Carole, and Blanca was glad to see that he was once again the father she knew so well, that what had happened to him was just a temporary condition.

But later, as he continued to speak, he began to talk about another injustice, much graver and unknown to her, that had caused him great sorrow and blocked his way in life. He declared that when the time came he would bring a lawsuit against that good-for-nothing. Blanca tried to find out more about that injustice, and who the man was who had committed it. But as he plunged deeper and deeper into the details, Blanca realized that her beloved father had lost his way in dark labyrinths and was trying with all his strength to extricate himself.

On their way back to the old age home, he continued to speak angrily against everyone who had stood in his way. His face grew taut, and his words burned. When they parted, he said, "Go in peace, my daughter. It's good that you at least are happy in life." All the way home, Blanca tried to hold back her tears.

18

BLANCA HAD PLANNED to go to Himmelburg the next day but didn't. Bad dreams tormented her during the night, and when she woke up it seemed to her that she must stay at home. She made a cup of coffee, heard the train leave, and with every sip of the beverage she knew that a part of her body had stopped pulsing, that from now on she would have to live an amputated life. That feeling traveled down into her legs, and she curled up in the armchair. She sat there, without moving, for a long time.

Later she recovered and went outside. The sky was bright, and the thought that she was still left with a few days to be by herself made her so happy that the memory of her father was effaced. Without locking the door, she headed for the center of town. Not far away students gaily strolled to the high school. It was Wednesday, she recalled. On Wednesdays studies began at ten o'clock, a kind of minor midweek holiday. A distant, hidden holiday feeling returned to her.

The stores downtown were open, and a pleasant morning bustle filled the narrow streets. Blanca liked that hour. In the past, on vacations, she used to go to the store and pull her father into the nearby café, which was called My Corner. They would sit for a while, immersed in conversation. Spending time with her father was an adventure that always thrilled her: a time of dreams and more dreams.

Blanca entered the café. It was old-fashioned, filled with warm, pleasant-looking furniture. The proprietors, a childless couple, had converted to Christianity in their youth, hoping that their life in the city would change for the better and that their business would flourish. But the café didn't flourish. A few customers, regulars, remained faithful to the place, but the young people took no interest in the old-fashioned, dark atmosphere that prevailed there. Years of disappointment had left their mark on the owners' faces. They had come to resemble each other, shrunken, and the light in their eyes had dimmed. But they had liked Blanca's father and greatly honored him, making him coffee very punctiliously. The proprietress, Mrs. Hofmann, used to say, "We'll hear great things of Blanca." That pronouncement would bring a thin smile to her father's lips, because he secretly hoped so, too.

"Where's Papa? I haven't seen him in a long time," asked Mrs. Hofmann.

"He's in the old age home in Himmelburg." Blanca didn't hide the information from them.

"Good God!" said Mrs. Hofmann, covering her face with her hands.

"I would gladly keep him at home, but Adolf won't allow it."

"Why? After all, he's a quiet, pleasant man."

"Adolf doesn't like Jews," said Blanca, shocked at the sentence that had escaped her.

The Hofmanns gave her a frozen look, without adding a word.

Again Blanca stood on the main street. The broad doorway of the locked synagogue was vacant. Grandma Carole would arrive there later. The day before, Blanca had thought of going to her house, to tell her about her father's sad situation and ask her to remove her curse from him. For some reason she thought that only Grandma Carole had the power to help her. She had lain in bed for a long time, trying to cobble together some words that would soften Grandma Carole's anger, but in the end Blanca realized her grandmother wouldn't help her, not because of hostility toward her father, but because of what she, Blanca, had done. It would be better not to go to her.

Blanca knew everyone downtown. Still, it seemed to her that the center of town had changed. Her mother had brought her to kindergarten here and later to elementary school. When she was little, her mother would take her to the town's seamstress, a Czech woman. Love of humanity dwelled in her face.

"We're together for such a short time," she used to say. "It's a shame to waste that time with misunderstandings and annoyance." She would take measurements and chat at the same time. She spoke about Prague and the charm of its streets, and she told them a lot about the Jews of Prague. She had worked for a long time—until her late marriage—for Jews.

"The Jews are the leavening in the dough," she would say. "Without the Jews, the world would be missing a spice."

Blanca remembered her very clearly. When she was seven, the dressmaker passed away. For some reason her mother took her to the funeral. It was a silent funeral, without tears. Only her mother couldn't restrain herself and wept.

Blanca raised her eyes and saw the closed synagogue again. Her father hadn't liked the place and used to say, "The synagogue lacks beauty. Jews don't pray, they mumble. In church at least there's good music." Her mother attended services on Rosh Hashanah and Yom Kippur. She had brought Blanca to services a few times. The women's section was roomy and vacant. In a single dark corner a handful of women crowded together, listening to the prayers that rose from the main sanctuary. Blanca was frightened by the place, but she still accompanied her mother.

After a while the synagogue was closed because there was no

longer a congregation. The tall, empty building stood out even more in its barrenness. If it had sunk, everyone would have been relieved, but a solid building like that never sinks by itself. Over the years it became a temple for a single worshipper of God: Grandma Carole.

When Blanca was a little girl, Judaism had appeared to her as a kind of severe disease, accompanied by fever and vomiting. Once she had spoke about this to her mother, who had replied with a sentence that was deeply engraved in her memory.

"I don't make a business out of my Judaism," she had said, "but I'm not ashamed of it, either." That was before tuberculosis had attacked her. When she was ill and lying in a rest home, she had said something to Blanca by chance: "Jews suffer everywhere."

"Why, Mama?"

"Because they're sensitive."

"More sensitive than other people?" Blanca had challenged her.

"No. Just weaker."

"Strange," Blanca had said.

"What's so strange?" her mother had asked.

"That Jews are weaker."

"That's how things are."

Blanca remembered that conversation with great clarity, perhaps because it had taken place in the evening. Her father was sitting in the armchair, and her mother had spoken slowly, as though counting her words.

19

AS BLANCA WAS returning home toward evening, from a distance she saw a man standing in front of her door and knocking on it. First it seemed to her that it was Karl, the church beadle, who used to make the rounds before the holidays, soliciting contributions for the church. When she drew nearer, he looked to her like Dachs, her father's former partner. But when she was only a few feet away from her house, she saw in amazement that it was her father.

"Papa!" she called out loud.

"I came back," said her father. A frightened and perplexed look had hardened on his long, narrow face.

"What's the matter?" Something of his frozen voice clung to her.

"I missed home," he said, smiling.

Now she saw: he was thin, and his posture was stooped. It was as if he had left his earthly existence in Himmelburg and had brought here only his trembling soul.

Blanca hugged him and gathered him to her heart. "How good it is that you've come back," she said.

"I didn't know what to do," said her father, covering his mouth with his right hand.

"Let's go to My Corner."

"We'll sit in your house. Why go so far?" he said, as though seeking cover.

"Everything is neglected in the house. And there isn't anybody in My Corner at this hour."

They set off for the center of town and Blanca did most of the talking, telling him about everything that had happened to her since the morning. Her father wasn't distracted. He listened attentively, as though she were telling him secrets. When they reached the center of town, it was already three o'clock. The sun flooded the shop windows with cool light. Her father raised his eyes, as though looking away from a terrible dream, and said, "I'm so glad I came back. It's good to return to your native city."

Blanca was alarmed by that sentence.

"I have no special sentiments for this city," she said. "There are more important things than the city you live in."

"What are they?" He surprised her.

"A good feeling, for example," she said, and she was pleased that she hadn't been tripped up in an idle statement.

"True, the evening light is always joyful," he said, pausing, as though he weren't sure of what he'd said.

"I feel no sentiments for this city. I would gladly travel to another place."

"Where?" he asked with his old curiosity.

"To Vienna, for example."

"I," he said, returning to his former ways, "find our city very pleasant."

This was not the ill and confused father whom Blanca and Adolf had put into the old age home but, rather, the father from her childhood. He had always dreamed. Her mother loved him because he was a dreamer, and when he failed—he mainly failed—she would support him with her fragile body and envelop him with soft speech, with good food, with a new coat that she had bought him. Or she would take him out for a long walk. She was his great admirer, and she believed in his hidden talents, which would someday be discovered.

"So, where shall we sit, Papa?"

This time her father preferred Amnon & Tamar to My Corner. They sat in the place where they always sat, near the window, across from the acacia tree, whose leaves had fallen, revealing its sturdy trunk. They ordered coffee and cheesecake, and the waiter, who had known them for many years, said, "It's been a long time since I've seen you, sir. How are you?"

"Everything's as it should be."

"Thank God," said the waiter, withdrawing to the counter.

Blanca's father didn't say a single word about Himmelburg. He spoke about a few efforts he had made in the past to extricate himself from the difficulty of earning a living. Once he had even gone to Vienna, where he had been offered the management of a small bookstore. The offer fell through because the salary they offered him would barely cover his rent. Her mother was prepared to do any kind of work to pull him out of that swamp, but her father wouldn't agree, and the idea was shelved.

He went on for a bit, and Blanca said, "Let's take a walk in the direction of the station."

"I don't want to go back to Himmelburg. That place depresses me."

"Where will we sleep?" Blanca spoke in the plural.

"I," he said in a voice that froze her, "am returning to my home."

"Papa."

"What's the matter?"

"We don't have a home. We sold the house. Don't you remember?"

"We sold our house?"

"Yes, Papa. We had debts."

"I don't want to go back to Himmelburg. That dark place depresses me." He spoke the way he had sometimes spoken when her mother was alive.

"I'd invite you to stay with us, but my house, Papa, is completely full. Adolf's sister and her three children live with us," she lied.

"Don't you have a bed for me?"

"Everything is dirty, crowded, and noisy." She spoke hurriedly.

"I don't know what to do," he said, cracking his knuckles.

"Let's take a walk. Don't you want to take a walk?"

Now she tried to entertain him, to distract him and lead him indirectly back to the railway station. Amazingly, she managed.

She told him that after Adolf's sister left the house and returned to her own home, she intended to enroll in a course in bookkeeping.

"But you wanted to study at the university, didn't you?"

"Later, Papa."

"And what does Adolf say?"

"He's very encouraging."

"I'm glad. Your happiness is very precious to me. I never managed to accomplish anything."

Now he spoke about himself again, about his partner, Dachs, and about his classmates who were weak students and became successful industrialists.

"How can you explain that, Papa?"

"Abstract thought isn't good for commerce." Again he surprised her with a clear and accurate insight.

"And what's needed for success?"

"A certain kind of coarseness of mind."

Now she was alarmed by the clarity of his thought.

They reached the station on time. Blanca had intended to join him, to stay overnight in Himmelburg and return the following day, but her father said quietly, in his customary tone of voice, "Why displace yourself at night? Sleep in your own bed, and come to visit me tomorrow."

"Still, I want to join you."

"There's no need, dear."

Now he no longer tarried but walked up the steps into the railroad car and sat at the window. The car was empty, and Blanca managed to see him in profile. Then the train began to move, and Blanca waved good-bye with both hands.

Surprisingly, her father opened the window and called out, "Thank you very much, Blanca. It was a wonderful day."

The train quickly moved off into the distance, and Blanca's face flooded with tears.

20

THE NEXT MORNING, the postman woke Blanca and handed her a telegram.

"Your father disappeared last night," it read. "Police and citizens searching for him. Come at once." At first it seemed as though the old postman had risen up out of her nightmares, but she saw her error immediately. He was Richard, the postman she had known since her childhood. At one time he delivered the mail in the center of town. Later he was transferred to the outlying areas.

"Papa's disappeared," Blanca said, hardly knowing what she was saying.

The postman's jaw dropped. "Where was he?" he asked.

"He was here. I accompanied him to the Himmelburg train. He was pleased. We had spent time together downtown."

"Why did he go to Himmelburg?"

"He's living in the old age home."

"All kinds of strange things happen in old age homes," said the elderly man. He closed his bag and stood where he was.

"What can I do?" Blanca asked distractedly. Now she saw her father's face clearly in the train window. Before getting on the train, he had spoken quietly and cogently, as though he understood that there was no way out and that he had to go back.

It was ten o'clock, and a pure autumn sun stood in the sky.

"Blanca," said the postman in a fatherly voice. "Get dressed. The train leaves in an hour."

"Yes," she said, as though he had woken her up again.

"People don't get lost." He used a peasant proverb to calm her fears and then went on his way.

Blanca dressed quickly and hurried to the station. There was no one there, and the young conductor made a joke at her expense. He heaped compliments on her and then casually mentioned that he had seen Adolf in the bar at the training center the day before.

"How is he?" Blanca asked.

"Don't worry. There are plenty of girls there."

For the first time in her life, she felt disgust.

There was no commotion in the old age home. It was twelve thirty, and the inmates were lying in bed. Her father's bed was unmade, and it was evident to Blanca as she approached that many hands had disturbed it.

"What happened?" she asked.

"Last night your father disappeared," said the man in the neighboring bed, and he sat up.

"Where did he disappear to?"

"I don't know," he replied, shrugging his shoulders.

"Strange," she said, and she knew that wasn't the appropriate word.

"Are they unkind to the inmates here?" she asked.

"No, never," said the old man, smiling. He quickly added, "We don't bother anyone, and no one bothers us."

From the director, Blanca learned that her father's footprints led to the nearby grove. The janitor and two cleaning women immediately went out to look for him. The police had arrived, and they, too, were looking. The weather was fair, and that would help them locate him. The director sounded satisfied, as if she had succeeded in doing what was necessary at that time.

"Do a lot of people go to the woods?" Blanca asked cautiously.

"Not many, but every year one or two of the inmates disappear. In the end we find them." She tried to soothe Blanca.

"I'll go and have a look myself," Blanca said, and she went out

into the rear courtyard. The broad, empty courtyard was illuminated by a dull noon light. The gate was open, and it seemed as if it
had been that way for years. It was decorated with metal ornaments
and had evidently known better days.

No one was to be seen in the nearby grove. There was just a
cold, motionless silence. The idea that her father had left his bed
at night and gone out into these woods began to seem more con-
crete to her. Now she remembered that he would occasionally get
angry, and harsh words would escape from his mouth. Usually it
was because of something connected to the store, the source of his
torments. Once, in a terrible moment of anger, he came up close
to his partner, Dachs, and shouted, "Monster!" But his greatest
hatred was for Grandma Carole. She was the thorn in his flesh.
Because of Blanca's grandmother, he didn't even go to synagogue
on Yom Kippur. He attended funerals bareheaded, and he signed
a petition demanding the closing of the kosher butcher because
Jewish ritual slaughter was cruel. This soft-spoken, courteous man,
whom everyone liked, would be filled with fury every time anyone
mentioned Grandma Carole's name. Once he had gone too far.
"All my misfortunes have befallen me because of her," he said. Now
his angry face was turned toward his daughter. Blanca returned to
the old age home.

The old people gathered around her and asked whether there was
any news. Blanca told them she was considering going to the police
and asking them to deploy as many men as possible in the area.
The nights were cold, and her father wasn't dressed properly. The
old people agreed with her.

Meanwhile, lunch was being served, and Blanca was offered a
bowl of soup. She sipped the hot liquid and told everyone about
the mailman who had awakened her that morning. She recounted
this dispassionately, as though what had happened to her was only
a nightmare. Now that it had passed, she could tell others about it.

The old people stared at her. "What can we do?" they asked.

"I won't give the police any respite." Blanca spoke in a voice not her own.

The kitchen worker brought her a second course as well. Now most of the old people were sitting in the dining room, eating and drinking from ornate ceramic mugs that didn't look as though they belonged to the place. Blanca repeated that she intended to go to the police, ask for an interview with the chief inspector, and explain the urgency of the matter to him. The nights were cold and dark, and a person who had lost his way was liable to fall into a pit. One of the old men made a dismissive gesture with his hand and looked at her skeptically, as if to say, *They won't do a thing, I know.*

Suddenly these strangers surrounding her had become the only close relatives Blanca had in the world, and for a moment she thought about telling them everything that had happened to her since she had married Adolf.

"Why did he go back to Heimland?" one of the old men asked, interrupting her thoughts.

"He missed his home," she said, and was appalled by the words that had left her mouth.

"He shouldn't have gone back. If you are doomed to be in an old age home, you should just stay there, without moving. No one will have mercy on you."

Blanca was about to reply that her father had in fact gone to ask for shelter in her home, but that she was afraid of Adolf. Adolf couldn't stand her father. He used to call him a weakling, subject to moods, someone who didn't know how to work. She wanted to tell them that she was afraid to bring her father into her home, fearing that Adolf would beat her for it, for he would beat her mercilessly. She intended to say all that, but she didn't have the courage to do so. She just repeated that she was going to go to the police and ask them to send out more men that night, because the nights were very cold and dark.

21

AT THE POLICE STATION Blanca learned that the two patrolmen who had been summoned to the Jewish old age home that morning went out right away, gathered testimony, and submitted a report.

"Didn't they search anymore?" Blanca asked.

"Where are we to look for him, madam?" the officer in charge said. A sharp laugh, like that of someone who had seen reversals in his life, burst from his thick lips.

"I'm sorry," said Blanca.

"If we knew where he was, we would go out and get him. We have a total of three policemen in this town. Two of them patrol, and one sits here. We relieve one another every few hours. In this town, for our sins, there are quite a few thefts."

"I don't know what to do," Blanca said, and she really didn't. Her head felt like a void, as though all the thoughts in it had been uprooted, leaving only the walls.

Seeing her helplessness, the policeman looked at the report that lay before him and said, "I see that your father was in Heimland yesterday. What was he doing in Heimland?"

"He came to visit me. He missed the town," Blanca answered hurriedly, glad that the words left her mouth in that order.

"And when did he return to Himmelburg?"

"On the last train," she said, hoping that would be an end to the questions.

"And who accompanied him to the train?"

"I did," Blanca said with a feeling of relief.

"Old people usually don't like to go back at night," the policeman remarked in a matter-of-fact way.

"True."

"So why did he return at night?"

"He wanted to return."

"I understand," he said.

"I offered to accompany him, but he said he wanted to go back alone."

"Was he in a bad mood during the past few days?"

"He was a little depressed in the old age home," Blanca said, sensing that the policeman was starting to rummage through her private life.

Indeed, he didn't let up.

"He's fifty-three years old, I see. What's a fifty-three-year-old man doing in an old age home?"

"He had no home. He had to sell his house."

"And why didn't he live with you?" It was an arrow fired directly at her forehead.

"My husband absolutely opposed it," Blanca said, the words sticking in her throat.

"Is your father sick?"

"No."

"So why did your husband refuse to keep him in your home?"

Blanca burst into tears.

The policeman stopped his questioning.

"I didn't have the strength to stand up to him," she muttered.

"There's nothing to worry about," he said, now trying to console her. "Every day people disappear and then reappear the following day. That's how the world works. How long has he been living in the old age home?"

"Three weeks, no more."

"Every month somebody runs away from there, usually new residents. But don't worry, they come back. They have no choice. The cold at night forces them to come back."

"A lot of people run away from the old age home?" For a moment she tried to meld her voice into his.

"Quite a few. They also run away from the Catholic old age home."

"And you look for them?" She forgot that she had already asked this.

"How is it possible to look for them?" he replied. "After all, this is a far-flung region, with groves, forests, swamps, and whatnot. If someone wants to run away, the hand of the law won't touch him. We don't even find murderers, unless they give themselves up voluntarily."

"I didn't know."

"That's how it is in this region. I don't know whether it's different in other places."

"What can I do, sir? What do you advise me to do now?"

"Not to do anything. That's my advice."

"And he'll come back?"

"He will certainly come back. He went out wearing his street clothing, it says in the report, which means that he can survive for three nights. My advice: go home and wait for him to come back." His rough face was filled with a simple humanity, as though he weren't a policeman, but someone in whom much wisdom of life was stored up.

"He'll come back, sir?"

"I'm sure he'll come back," he said, and rose to his feet.

"My heartfelt thanks," she said, and bowed her head.

Blanca didn't immediately realize what the policeman had done to her. Only later, as she sat in a tavern downing drink after drink, did she understand that this stranger, without the superior airs of a judge, had laid her shame before her eyes and made her see that her father had fled because she hadn't taken him into her home and he didn't want to live in the old age home. That sharp insight burned her eyes, and she closed them. But the pain kept spreading. In vain she tried to dull it with cognac. But every sip merely heightened her awareness, and her pain.

22

WHEN BLANCA RETURNED to the old age home, it was already evening. In answer to her question about whether her father had come back, one of the inmates answered loudly, "Erwin didn't return."

Blanca went over to her father's bed and made it. Contact with the blankets reminded her of her mother's dried-out face. During the last months of her life, a heartbreaking spirituality radiated from her.

"Don't worry about me," she kept saying. "I'm absolutely fine." She apparently felt the end coming and tried to cover her weakness with her last remaining strength. During her final days, she was alert, remembered many details, and wasn't confused about dates. She resembled someone preparing for a long journey, unafraid for her own body.

One of the workers roused Blanca from her memories.

"Come, Blanca, and eat something," she said. "We have a summer squash quiche. You'll like it."

"Thank you. I must go."

"Where?"

"I have to get home. I live far away."

"Happiness doesn't await you at home," said the woman with a simple directness.

"How do you know?" Blanca wondered.

"From my body," said the woman.

Blanca lowered her eyes. The woman took her by the arm and led her to the kitchen. The kitchen was in disarray. A blackened pot stood on the sooty stove, and it was clear that the pot had belonged to that stove for many years. The woman sat Blanca down at a table, served her a bowl of soup, and said, "Eat this first. It will warm you up."

Blanca realized that no one had served her with such attention since her mother's death. She raised her eyes and looked closely at the unfamiliar woman. She was short and full-figured, and her head was planted on her shoulders as if she had no neck. She wore a stained blue shirt, and it was evident that she was hardworking and liked to serve people the food she had cooked.

Unaware of what she was doing, Blanca rolled up her sleeve and said, "I have a wound that won't heal. Perhaps you have a bandage."

"I certainly do," the woman said and hurried to the first-aid cupboard. When she returned, she fell to her knees and cleaned the wound with a cloth.

"That's an ugly wound," she said. "Who hit you?"

"Don't ask."

"I used to be beaten sometimes, too. Now he's sick," she said, revealing a mouth in which only a few teeth were left.

"You, too?" Blanca looked up, suddenly recognizing in her a sister in suffering.

"Indeed."

"What did you do?"

"What could I do? I tried to stay far from home."

"And when would you return home?"

"Only once a week, to give him the money. Here no one does you any harm. You sleep comfortably."

"How many years have you been working here?"

"It's been twenty years now."

"And he always hit you?"

"Always."

When Blanca finished the soup, the woman served her a portion of the squash quiche and said, "You'll like this."

Blanca was hungry, and the hunger made her forget the turmoil of the day. A half-remembered warmth enveloped her.

"You have to find yourself work in an old age home, far from the house. You're still young, and you mustn't give in."

"Thank you," said Blanca, feeling that the woman was speaking with a guileless heart.

"If you feel like having a fellow at night, you'll find one here, too. A man for one night will always spoil you. I'm speaking the truth. I'm no liar."

Blanca chuckled.

"Why are you laughing?"

"There's truth to what you say."

"In the old age home you're like a princess. The old people are good-hearted, and if they have a penny, they'll give it to you. They aren't stingy."

"Thanks," Blanca said, and tears welled up in her eyes.

"You mustn't be stupid."

Blanca bit her lip and brushed away her tears. "Can I get a job here?" she asked.

"Here they've run out of money. They haven't paid us our salaries for the past few months. But in Blumenthal, which is nearby, there's a nice, well-organized old age home. Much nicer than this one. The old people are wealthy, and they shove banknotes into your hand every time you approach their beds. You're still young. You should go to Blumenthal."

"You're kind to me. What's your name?"

"My name is Theresa."

"Mine is Blanca."

"Women suffer everywhere. Why didn't you marry a Jew?"

Theresa's comment surprised her.

"I don't know."

"You can't cry over spilt milk," Theresa said, and gave her another serving of squash.

"I thank you from the bottom of my heart," Blanca said, rising from her chair. "Now I have to go home. My husband is coming back from an occupational training course, and if I don't make him a good meal, he'll hit me."

"They always go off to training courses," said Theresa, laughing.

"Why are you laughing?"

"That's what they call their bashes. My husband also used to say he was going to a training course. They come back fired up like randy horses."

"What do they do there?"

"They get drunk and screw peasant women."

"And that's what they call a training course arranged by the factory?"

"Yes. Didn't you know?"

Theresa dear, I now have no one at all in the world, Blanca was about to say. *I'll stay here. I'll wait for my father to come back. I'm afraid to go home.*

Theresa seemed to guess Blanca's thoughts. "You have to go home now," she said. "Prepare the house as if nothing has happened, and the first chance you get, go to Blumenthal. The old age home in Blumenthal is splendid."

"And he'll let me go?"

"If you bring home money, he'll let you. They desire money more than women. The main thing is not to be afraid. Those who are afraid are punished doubly. You have to say to yourself, *Nothing will frighten me anymore. If I have to die, I'll die, but I won't be afraid.* Fear, my dear, is our ruin. Fear is our enemy. The moment you free yourself from fear, you'll be a new person, you'll be free and your movements will be free. You'll walk in the street with your back straight."

"Thank you, Theresa."

"Don't thank me. Do what I told you to do."

"And that will take away my fear?"

"Without a doubt."

Blanca took Theresa's words in like the soup she had served her earlier. Her entire body was filled with the events of the day. It was already dark, and she went to the station like someone whose fears had been drugged.

23

ADOLF RETURNED THE next day, and when Blanca asked him how he had enjoyed the Tyrolean Mountains, he answered, "We didn't enjoy ourselves. We worked hard." Blanca served him roasted meat, cabbage, and baked potatoes. He was hungry and asked for seconds. When he took off his shirt, she was astonished to see how solid he was. His arms appeared to belong to another race of men.

Later she told him that her father had disappeared the previous day and that she had been summoned by the old age home in Himmelburg. He didn't respond, but when she went on to tell him about everything that had happened to her, he said, "That's the Jewish muddle-brain." When he finished the meal, he lit a cigarette and said, "You don't have to go back there. It's a rotten place."

Blanca remembered that right after her mother died, Adolf had said, "Jews don't know how to live, and they don't know how to die." She had been overcome with grief, and that surprising comment had struck her like a hammer. Now she remembered exactly when he had said it: right after the funeral, at the gate to the cemetery. That evening he had made some general statements about the Jews, statements with which she concurred in her heart. If he had said them quietly, without poison, she would have agreed with him completely. At that time she was dreaming about changing herself in a way that would infuse her life with patience and calm. Her arms would swell to the size of Adolf's sisters', her body would harden and broaden, her chest would fill out, and she would be able to work without her back bothering her. Adolf insisted that she change herself and said that if she didn't do so of her own free will, he would change her by force. And that was indeed how he behaved. He beat her with his hands and with his belt, and did not lack for occasions to do so. *Great God,* she whispered to herself, *why is my life so painful?* Her bereaved, confused father was so immersed in his own misfortune, he didn't see his daughter's pain. She learned to close her eyes and keep silent, to bite her lips and not utter a syllable. Sometimes, when she could bear no more, she would plead, "Don't hit me. You're hurting me." But Adolf paid no attention.

"You're a weakling," he would say. "You have no muscles. You're shouting like your crazy grandmother." Sometimes it seemed to her that he didn't mean to hurt her but, rather, to uproot her weakness. He said he would destroy everything that she once was. In an effort to improve herself, she would slave away and say to herself, *Adolf is right, I must get stronger. Only a strong person stands on his own two feet. Weak people fail in the end.*

Adolf's absence had made her body forget slightly the pain he inflicted on her. Now everything reverted to the way it had been, but in a harsher way, as if he had left only to gather more rage.

Blanca's father's disappearance came to appear to her as a voyage to the realm of his youth: his love of mathematics. Now, in his hiding place, he had become again what he once was: a genius. There he was planning his great discoveries: his marvelous equations, about which he had been thinking for years. As soon as the equations were known, all the humiliations would be erased in a single moment, and he would be what he was meant to be: the genius who was going to bring a blessing to the world. *Papa,* she would say to herself, *I can guess where you're hiding, but I won't disturb you. You're preparing the final draft, and victory will not be slow in coming.*

But Blanca also had moments of dreadful mental clarity, and

she knew that no garment could cover the shame, that no words would atone for her crime. That evening in the railroad station— God would not forgive her for it. To dull her hidden pains Blanca would work from morning till night, baking and cooking, but Adolf was not content. There were always faults: the potatoes were burned, the roast was dry, the vegetables weren't properly seasoned. He spent the evenings with his friends in the tavern, and upon his return he would peel off her clothes, beat her, and mount her.

"Don't hurt me," she would plead. But her pleas would only make his fury burn hotter.

I'll run away, she said to herself more than once, *and no one will know where I've disappeared to. I'll live among the bulrushes or on the edge of the hills. Better to live in the forest than to endure this shameful suffering.* The desire would burn brightly within her, but fear would put it out. Her secret plans eventually shrank to something more reasonable. *I'll sneak away to Himmelburg and find out what has happened with the searches for my father. If I learn that he is living in the mountains, I'll go to him, no matter what.*

As the autumn rains pelted down in fury, Blanca hurriedly put on her raincoat and went to the railway station. By nine o'clock she was in Himmelburg. The familiar houses and the road to the old age home made her dizzy. For a moment she forgot why she had come, and she went into a café. The strong coffee refreshed her memory, and she recalled that she had been there three weeks earlier. It had been cold, but no rain was falling. The courtyard had been lit, and a motionless silence had filled it. She had spoken with the director and gone to the police, and when she had returned, Theresa had served her soup and summer squash quiche.

After sitting for an hour, Blanca gathered herself up and went to the old age home. She went in through the main entrance and headed for the corridor where her father had lain. When she reached his bed, she saw an unfamiliar old man in his place, his eyes sunk in dark sockets and his face hardened. *What are you doing here?* she was about to call out. *This is my father's bed. You can't just grab a bed like that. If he comes back today, where will he sleep?*

The director's face was blank and inspired no hope. When Blanca asked whether there was any point in going back to the police, she replied, "My dear, what can I tell you? They do what they want. I bribe them, but it's useless. God has died in their hearts."

"Where did he disappear to?" Blanca suddenly asked, as though he had been gone for just a day.

"Who knows?" answered the director, alarmed by Blanca's question.

Theresa was more open.

"They wait for seven days," she said, "and if after seven days the person doesn't return, that means he'll never return, that he decided of his own free will to go to the world of truth. He had enough of the confusion and the lies and the suffering that disfigures us. I've been working here for twenty years. It's never happened that someone has come back after a long absence." Her voice had a grave and direct quality, like that of someone who has decided not to conceal the truth, even if it's cruel.

Blanca drew near to her. "Have we lost all hope?"

"One mustn't deceive people. I hate deceivers. Death isn't as horrible as we imagine it to be."

Blanca held out her hand, as though trying to cut her off, but Theresa wouldn't stop.

"The next world is better," she said, as she went to get Blanca a bowl of soup. "Believe me."

"Thank you, but I have to return home," said Blanca. "Adolf comes home at three thirty, sometimes even at three. If his meal isn't ready, he'll beat me."

"Just don't be afraid, my dear."

"I'm not afraid anymore," Blanca said, and hugged her.

"You mustn't despair. We aren't alone. There's a God in heaven."

"I know," said Blanca, and she ran out to catch the noon train.

24

THAT VERY WEEK Blanca discovered she was pregnant. Fear seized her, and her body trembled. She didn't tell Adolf a thing. Adolf kept on teaching her lessons, being angry with her and beating her. She would hold her breath and say to herself, *If he knew I was pregnant, he would let up.* She worked diligently in the house and in the garden. It seemed to her that if she worked hard and devotedly, she would placate him.

On Sundays his parents would come, and his brothers and sisters would cram into the house until there was no more room. The odor of beer would make her head spin, but Blanca tried to overcome that weakness as well. She would repeat to herself, *Real life isn't soft the way it was in my parents' house, but thick and solid. Anyone who doesn't understand that is laboring under a delusion.* Now she tried to eat the way Adolf did, to sleep on her back the way he did, and to grow brown skin, but her body, to her misfortune, didn't comply. Dizzy spells would attack her at times, and at night she would wake up and vomit. Finally, she told him she was pregnant.

"Pregnancy's not a disease," he responded.

"So why am I vomiting?"

"My sisters were pregnant, and they didn't vomit."

"Be merciful to me." The words escaped from her lips.

"What's the matter with you?"

"I feel abandoned."

"What are you talking about?"

Once a week she would sneak off to Himmelburg. Now it was her secret shelter. The director of the old age home had fallen ill meanwhile, and she lay in a narrow bed like one of the inmates. The welfare office of the Jewish community in Vienna promised to send a substitute director, but she was slow in arriving. From her sickbed, the director mumbled orders that could barely be understood. Theresa was now, in fact, the director. She fought with the cleaning women and with the suppliers, who threatened to sue the old age home for accumulated debts.

"Go ahead!" Theresa would say to them. "If they put the old people in prison, they'll be better off. I'm prepared to go with them, too." Blanca helped do laundry, clean the floors, and feed the weak residents. That exhausting work outside of her home brought her some relief, and every time she was able to escape, she did.

On one of her fleeting visits she told Theresa, "I'm pregnant."

"Don't expect any special treatment" was Theresa's immediate reaction.

"He'll keep beating me, even now?"

"He'll keep on."

"And what about the baby?"

"Protect it with both hands. That's all you can do, no more."

"Who would have thought?" said Blanca, covering her face with her hands.

One morning Adolf caught her at the train station buying a ticket at the window. Blanca froze on the spot and fainted. The people standing in line rushed to wash her face with water and call the medic. Adolf stood there like an oppressor, without taking his eyes off her. When she roused from her faint, he asked, "Where were you planning to go?"

"To Himmelburg."

"What do you have there?"

"I wanted to look for my father."

"Bitch," he hissed.

She knew the end would be bitter, but where and when, she didn't reckon. She felt heavy and shackled, as though in a nightmare, and with no way out. Everywhere she turned, the gate was shut in her face. Finally, having no other option, she spoke to her mother-in-law and begged for her mercy. Blanca's mother-in-law didn't like her. When she saw Blanca for the first time, she had fixed her with a hostile gaze, and that gaze had not changed over time. She regarded Blanca as a woman who was not engaged in life.

"Adolf beats me," Blanca said.

A thin smile spread across her mother-in-law's face, as though this were a trivial misdemeanor.

"I'm afraid for the baby that's in my womb." Blanca sought a different kind of mercy.

The smile left her mother-in-law's face all at once. "Every decent husband hits a little. Nobody dies from it."

"I'm not used to it," said Blanca.

"You have to get used to it," her mother-in-law said, as though they were talking about a type of housework. "Jews spoil their girls. That kind of spoiling is despicable, and one mustn't become addicted to it."

Blanca knew now that salvation would not come from her mother-in-law. Nevertheless, she bared her thigh and showed her the wound.

"You shouldn't show things like that," her mother-in-law said, shocked. "A husband who beats is a loving husband. That's what we say. A woman without a beating becomes wanton. A husband not only supports her, he also watches over her."

"I'm not used to it," Blanca repeated helplessly.

"You have to get used to our way of life. Among us, husbands beat their wives. There's nothing wrong with that. That's how to love a wife, too."

Blanca hung her head, and tears welled up in her eyes.

For a month she vomited. The vomiting weakened her, but she still rose early to clean the house and prepare breakfast for Adolf. Adolf kept saying, "When my sisters were pregnant, they didn't vomit. You should have a stiff drink, not tea. Among us, only sick people and old people drink tea."

Before long the bleeding began. Adolf brought the medic. He examined her and said, "A doctor must see her."

The next day, Dr. Nussbaum came. Dr. Nussbaum was one of the town's best-known doctors. After finishing his studies, he converted and began to work in the public hospital. Blanca knew him well. She had studied with his daughter, a thin and sensitive girl named Celia. Any excessive movement, not to mention any harsh sight, would overwhelm her with emotion and make her cry. Once, on a class trip, they had ended up on a farm where pigs were snorting. The squealing of the pigs, which were trying to escape the slaughterers' axes, amused the class. Celia, seeing the slaughterers, fainted, falling into what seemed to be a coma; for a long time they tried to rouse her from it. In the end they had to summon her father from the hospital, and he resuscitated her himself.

"Blanca," the doctor called out with fatherly fondness.

Hearing that familiar voice, Blanca burst into tears.

"Don't cry. Nobody's done anything to you," Adolf commented.

"I'd like to ask everyone present to leave the room," Dr. Nussbaum ordered.

When he asked her what had caused all the wounds on her body, Blanca answered, "I fell down. I wasn't careful."

Dr. Nussbaum was an experienced physician, and he knew what some men did to their wives. He didn't hold his tongue. "Animals," he said.

"We're going to put you in the hospital," he continued, and took her under his protection.

Adolf had come back into the room and was about to say something, but seeing the doctor's anger, he didn't dare.

Thus Blanca left her prison. Her pains were sharp and her weakness was great, but the people who surrounded her were kind and pleasant. Every morning she would wake up as if she were in her parents' home. "Mama," she said, "you sent me these good angels."

Dr. Nussbaum visited her twice a day, and when he was off duty, he would sit and converse with her. He had known her parents well and had just heard about her father's disappearance. "We were friends from youth," he said, burying his face in his hands. "How is it I knew nothing? How is it I didn't sense anything? Are they still looking for him?"

"Not anymore."

25

IN THE HOSPITAL, Blanca was cared for with great concern. Christina, the nurse, sat at her side and told her about her life. Her parents had died when she was a child, and she had been forced to go out and work at a young age. First she had worked as a practical nurse. The medical staff had valued her work and sent her to Vienna to study at the nursing school. That was her profession, and this was her home. Blanca noticed: her steps were quick, but her upper limbs were somewhat stiff. A pallor covered her face, and she looked like someone who had not seen sunlight for many days.

Adolf visited her once and didn't return. Her mother-in-law would visit her after church on Sunday. She brought Blanca apples that had grown in her garden and urged her to taste them. Here she seemed softer, maybe because of the green scarf she wore on her head, but she still preached a little, even here.

"A woman must learn to suffer," she said. "Suffering purifies her. In the end, the children grow up and submit to her discipline." It was evident she was speaking from her own experience, but her words sounded as if they were the priest's.

"How is Adolf?" Blanca asked.

"He's working. He works hard." She protected her son.

"Send him my greetings," she said, as though he were not her husband but a distant relative.

"He's working hard," his mother repeated.

Every time Dr. Nussbaum came to see her, he brought her a chocolate or some fruit. With the death of the senior physician, he had become the chief doctor. The public hospital was on the brink of the abyss. During the past two years it had been running on a deficit. There were many debts, the creditors threatened to bring a lawsuit, and the maintenance staff went on strike from time to time. Dr. Nussbaum struggled on every front, and his back was bent from the great burden.

"How is Celia?" Blanca asked, because she was certain she was studying at the university.

"She's been in a convent, my dear, for more than a year. My daughter is a mystery to me. I see her once a month, talk with her, and I don't understand a thing."

"Did it happen suddenly?"

"She was engaged and about to be married. A date was even set, and then she suddenly decided she wanted to be among the servants of God, and the engagement was canceled."

"Good God!" Blanca said. "We neglect the ones closest to us. I was so involved with myself during the past two years, I didn't see anything around me."

The next day, Celia came to visit her. Seeing her friend in a nun's habit, Blanca burst into tears.

"Why are you crying?" Celia asked softly.

"I don't know," said Blanca, wiping her eyes.

Blanca told Celia that since her mother's death, her life hadn't gone well. Her father had disappeared mysteriously, and Adolf didn't allow her to go to Himmelburg to keep searching for him.

"I actually do sneak out and go there," she said, "but I'm too afraid of what I might discover to ask anything. And now the pregnancy's not going well, either. And you?"

"I live in the convent in Stillstein, and I'm preparing to become a nun. What happened to your father?"

"I don't know; I can't tell you anything," said Blanca emotionally. "Papa was my handhold on this world, and I, in my great stupidity, in my great fear, lost him. He slipped out of my hands. Fear is our undoing. Fear makes me a person with no substance. I never learned to have courage, and without courage a person is dust and ashes. Do you understand?"

"Certainly I understand you."

"Life was bitter for my father, and I didn't know how to help him. Since my marriage, I've been afraid of every shadow. How is it in the convent? Are people frightened there as well?"

"I have only been there for a year," said Celia, bowing her head.

"Sometimes it seems to me that prayer would help me, but I don't know how to pray. My mother used to pray sometimes. When I was a little girl I used to watch her lips. I would say to myself, *If only I knew how to pray like Mama.*"

"I remember your mother, and sometimes I see her before my eyes."

"My mother went to her final rest without any complaint," Blanca said.

"I found a lot of books about Judaism in the convent library, and I read them constantly. That's strange, isn't it? Did you ever happen to hear of Martin Buber?"

"No. Never."

"In my room I have books about the Ba'al Shem Tov, including a very precious anthology. I'm sure you'd find it interesting."

"What is it about?"

"About faith, if I may make a generalization."

"I feel empty, like an abandoned vessel."

"Martin Buber's anthology gave me a lot of light."

"I'm so distracted, as if I were born without a nest."

"I'll bring you the anthology. You'll find value in it. Isn't that what we once used to say?"

"Thank you," said Blanca. "I don't know what's wrong with me."

26

LATER BLANCA'S PAIN grew more intense, and Dr. Nussbaum
gave her something for it. The pain did indeed die down a little,
but the medicine made her woozy. Then Christina sat by her side
and said something. Blanca didn't absorb what she said, but it
seemed to her that Christina's lips were moving in prayer. For a
moment she wondered about that prayer, and this made her faintly
recall small scraps of her childhood. When she was sick, her mother
used to sit next to her bed and observe her. Blanca would feel her
hovering gaze, and she would sigh in relief. Then, surprisingly, a
marvelous sort of contact would take place between her mother
and her. Blanca's hidden fears would fade all at once, and she knew
that her mother would always be with her. But the full joy would
come afterward, when she was recovering, a time that lasted many
days and was full of glowing little things, like games of dominoes
or cards, or books by Jules Verne. Her mother would read a chapter
and say, "Now we'll take a little break and nibble something. What
shall it be? Maybe we'll peel a pear."

The weakness would pass, and Blanca's appetite would return.
She even found a slice of bread and butter tasty. Later the quiet
hours would come, when nothing happened, just a feeling of pleasure and the happiness of light. While she was recovering, her
father would try to entertain her with mathematical puzzles. She
couldn't solve them, but her father would do so effortlessly, like a
magician. During those marvelous, brightly lit days, sharp, sudden
fears would sometimes strike her, and she knew that her pleasure
would not last long, that parting was inevitable. She would cry bit-
terly, and her mother would try in vain to console her.

These bright scraps of memory, which had been hidden within Blanca for many years, now appeared before her with new clarity. She opened her eyes, and Christina was sitting next to her. For some reason she thought Christina was Celia, and she said, "Celia?"

"How are you, Blanca? How do you feel?" Christina asked.

"I dreamed about my mother," said Blanca.

Blanca felt better, but Dr. Nussbaum didn't release her. Adolf came and stood at the door. In his work clothes, alongside the white iron bedsteads, he looked like one of the sturdy maintenance men who carried beds and chests of drawers to the upper floor.

"When are you coming back home?" He spoke in his mother's voice.

She had noticed: Adolf resembled his mother and was full of superstitions. Once she had been sure that only weak people were subject to moods, daydreams, and superstitions. Later she learned that Adolf was careful to avoid the number thirteen. He had nailed a horseshoe above the door of their house, and sometimes he would say, "My mother says that a gate that doesn't have a cross on it doesn't protect the house." At first she didn't believe her ears, but in time she conceded to herself that superstitions were held by strong people, too, and in fact they enhanced their strength.

Without a doubt, Adolf was his mother's son. His mother always protected him and spoke about his work in the dairy with admiration. His father loved him less, but through him Adolf belonged to the Hammer clan, which was known for its industry, religiosity, and devotion to family. All of these were, of course, merely fictions and wishful thinking. The family was full of drunkards, adulterers, cheaters, and idiots. But she had to learn all this painfully, over the years. Now she knew nothing but aches. *Don't release me,* she was about to say to Dr. Nussbaum, *I'm afraid to go back home.* But Dr. Nussbaum spoke first, telling Adolf, "Blanca will be with us until she regains her strength and her wounds are completely healed."

"I don't understand," said Adolf.

"What don't you understand?"

"My sisters gave birth at home, not in a hospital."

"So you're an expert in medicine, too, I see," he said and dismissed him.

27

OTTO AWOKE FROM a bad dream and shouted, "Mama, Mama!"

"What's the matter?"

"Somebody wanted to catch me."

"Who, dear?"

"A tall, strong man."

"It was just a bad dream."

"Why did he scare me so much?"

"Dreams are frightening."

"If dreams are nonsense, why are they frightening?"

"There's nothing to be afraid of. I'm with you, dear."

Blanca wrote without letup. She spent most of the night at the desk, struggling with the order of events, the words, and the clarity of the sentences. The fear that soon they would have to leave this protected place gave her no rest. To overcome her fear, she remained wakeful, watching over Otto's slumber and writing.

They had been here for six weeks now. The garden produced tomatoes, cucumbers, onions, and radishes, and there were also beds of lettuce and squash. In addition, the landlady brought them apples and pears from the orchard at her house. Her old age was passing quietly and her face glowed, leaving a pleasant feeling that stayed in the house for hours.

I'm very much afraid that quite soon we'll lose this hidden Garden of Eden, Blanca wrote in her notebook, *and we'll have to set out for a lengthy exile. When did I hear the word "exile" for the first time? The religion teacher, Dr. Kaltbrunner, used to put out his long arm and say, "Were it not for Adam, we would have remained in the Garden of Eden. Because of his sin, we were exiled." Why did I remember Dr. Kaltbrunner? He used to intimidate the class.* Blanca finished that sentence and lay the pen down on the notebook. She immediately sensed that Otto's eyes were wide open and that he was observing her.

"Why aren't you asleep, dear?"

"I'm waiting for the morning."

"The morning is still far off. Meanwhile you can close your eyes."

Otto didn't answer right away. He would absorb a sentence and take it in. That secret internalization usually took long minutes, and sometimes an hour or two. But the response would finally come. He had stopped asking about his father. Every day Blanca supplied his soul with new sights and words to erase his home from his memory. It generally worked. Nevertheless, sometimes someone's name or a place emerged. Blanca didn't flinch, but cut off his question and hurried to distract him. Fortunately, Otto didn't insist. He heard her voice and clung to it. Now, as she looked at him, it seemed to her that he had changed. His face had darkened and his gaze was concentrated. He could count to twenty without making a mistake. At the start of the trip, he had still shouted with Adolf's frightening voice, but on the train he had already calmed down, his voice was softer, and he stopped throwing things. On the train he learned to touch things gently, to move them carefully, and to observe them.

"When will we go?"

"In a little while, dear."

Otto noticed that his mother's behavior had changed; her expression was tense, and she stood at the window for a long time, listening.

"Are you afraid, Mama?"

"No, dear. Why would I be afraid?"

"It seemed to me you were."

Blanca felt that the place was no longer as quiet as it had been before. Two days earlier, a serious fight had broken out in the neighboring house. People gathered from all around, and there had been a commotion. The following day, gendarmes came and questioned the neighbors. Blanca woke Otto, and while it was still dark they went out to the riverbank.

Blanca felt that she had to leave, but it was hard for her to uproot herself. This bright place had restored so much life to her. In fact, it brought back everything that had died within her. Now the desire burned within her to sit and write extensively. But first she would cling to her mother and father. Those two marvelous souls had ended their short lives in this world as strangers. They didn't know how to soar up high, but the ground was also hard for them. They circled low, painfully hovering until they ascended to the heights. Now it seemed to her that her mother had disappeared like her father, because the funeral hadn't left from their home but from the building in the Jewish cemetery where her body had been ritually washed. When they returned home the bed lay unmade, as if her mother were about to come back to it. At the time, death had seemed to Blanca like a yawning abyss, and she had escaped to Adolf, sure that Adolf was the fortified castle over which death had no dominion. One day, even before converting, she had spoken to him about her fear of death. He had listened and said, "Strange what thoughts run around in your brain."

"Aren't you afraid?"

"Of whom?"

Adolf was the castle. *But he didn't know he was the castle,* Blanca said to herself, sure that she would be saved in his presence.

She was sorry that just now, when she had found a tunnel to her old life and the secret things that were being deciphered for her, she had to leave this place and resume her wandering. Who knew what awaited her and whether she would again be able to see what she saw now. Over the past days she had been tense, leaping from topic to topic, trying to manage. But one idea led to another, and things got mixed up. For that reason, she decided that first she had to finish writing the episode of Adolf, for Otto's sake. So that when the time came, he would know exactly what had happened and how. Until now she had ignored what was expected of her, but yesterday Otto had asked her about death again, and it was clear that the shadow was oppressing him.

"There is no death," Blanca said, surprising him.

"Really?"

"I'll always be with you, even if I'm not here. You can talk to me the way you're talking to me now."

"And is that how you talk to your mama?"

"Yes, exactly that way, my dear."

28

THE HOSPITAL'S SITUATION worsened, and most of the patients were sent home. Blanca was among the last to go. Adolf didn't greet her gladly and expressed his consternation about her appearance. During the past few weeks she had, indeed, recovered, but her knees were weak and her legs felt unsteady. But she made all his meals on time anyway. Adolf no longer slapped her face, but he still preached to her and criticized the way she roasted meat. Every word that came from his mouth struck her temples, and the fear that had receded throbbed within her once again.

The last few days had been very difficult for Dr. Nussbaum. The maintenance workers, who hadn't received their salaries, first gathered in the courtyard and then went up to the top floor and overturned tables and cabinets. Dr. Nussbaum pleaded with them to stop.

"Why are you being hard on the patients?" he asked. But his words were in vain.

Dr. Nussbaum had been struggling with the Ministry of Health and the local authorities for years, as well as soliciting donations from wealthy people and persuading the workers to be patient. Usually he had managed to do the impossible. Now he stood in the hospital entrance and with shame escorted out those who were leaving it.

"Come see me soon," he said to Blanca. She had intended to go to him on Friday, but then she remembered that on Sunday Adolf's parents and his brothers and sisters would be coming, and there were no refreshments in the house. She immediately rushed to the butcher, and on Sunday at noon she served everyone at the table dumplings filled with meat and sauerkraut. When her mother-in-law asked how she felt, Blanca answered, "Much better." At the end of the day, her head was spinning and she could barely drag herself to bed.

The next day, when Adolf came home his face was dark and angry. Blanca hurriedly served his meal, and he ate without complaining. Suddenly, without warning, he raised his voice and shouted, "Where are the pickled cucumbers?"

"I didn't manage to make them yet," Blanca answered promptly. Adolf rose to his feet, walked over to her, and slapped her. This time the slap wasn't hard, and she didn't fall down, but the words that he had kept in during the weeks that she hadn't been there poured out of him in a frightening torrent.

"All the doctors are Jews. All the illnesses are Jewish, and the lawyers who defend the doctors are Jews. You shouldn't learn from them. You have to be at home, not there. You get sicker in the hospital. A normal person doesn't go to the hospital unless they're amputating his leg. The Jews fill up the hospitals."

Blanca didn't open her mouth. In the past, every time she replied, his fury would increase, his face would turn a saffron color, and he would raise his huge, hairy arms. Almost without realizing it, Blanca covered her belly with her hands and hoped for mercy. But Adolf's mercy wasn't aroused.

Before Blanca was discharged, Dr. Nussbaum had written Adolf a letter summoning him to his office.

"You must know that we cared for your wife for three weeks," he said, "to heal the wounds that you inflicted with your own hands. You're supposed to speak to a woman, not beat her like an animal." Adolf was about to reply, but seeing the doctor's angry eyes, he kept his mouth shut. But when he came home, he didn't hold his tongue: "The Jews won't give me instructions about when to sleep with my wife." Blanca was afraid that he would pour his rage out on her, but, fortunately, he hurried off to the tavern that evening, and when he came home, he fell into bed.

Blanca, despite everything, grew stronger. She worked in the house and the garden. Adolf continued to pick on her, but he was careful not to hit her. Her mother-in-law would come to visit her, advising her about what to cook for Adolf and how.

"Adolf likes a hot meal at night," she would say. "He's like his father, a hot meal calms him down, and it should be a roast, with potatoes and sauerkraut. Sometimes it would be good to make him squash stuffed with chopped meat."

Thus the days passed. The sun was apparently good for Blanca, and her face became tan. After two hours of work in the garden, she would make herself a cup of coffee. Her thoughts grew narrower, and all her senses were now given over to the baby in her womb. Sometimes, in the middle of the day, she would suddenly be attacked by a feeling of dread, and she would remember Himmelburg. She would start to get dressed, but fear would paralyze her legs again, and she would stay bound to her place.

One morning Blanca overcame her fears and took the first train to Himmelburg. Since her last visit, the old age home had changed beyond recognition. The director had passed away, and Theresa had been appointed temporarily in her place. Theresa came out to greet Blanca and hugged her, and she immediately began telling her about her trials and the troubles of the home. In Blanca's father's bed there now slept a man whose sightless eyes were sunk deeply in their sockets; an involuntary smile fluttered on his lips. Theresa served Blanca a bowl of soup and asked her whether she had been to Blumenthal yet. Blanca told her that she had been in the hospital for the past month, and that upon going home she had found a neglected house and an angry husband.

"You still must go to Blumenthal. The old age home there is roomy and rich, and they'll greet you with open arms."

"And who'll take care of the baby?" Blanca wondered.

"A housekeeper. She'll give your husband some of her favors, and he'll be quieter and won't hit you as much. Your husband needs a beast of the field."

"How do you know that?" Blanca's eyes widened in surprise, as though Theresa had discovered a hidden secret.

"From my body, my dear. First my father beat me, then my husband. If you love life, you'll run away from there while your soul is still in you. If you don't, you'll be worn out and sick by the age of thirty. Spare yourself and get away from your house."

"I'm afraid."

"You mustn't be afraid. You have to say to yourself, 'There are more important things than fear, and I'll go to Blumenthal no matter what.'"

"Thank you, Theresa."

"Why thank me? We're sisters in suffering."

29

CELIA CAME TO visit Blanca the next morning, bringing Martin Buber's anthology of Ba'al Shem Tov stories. Blanca was glad to see her and hugged her. Now she noticed: Celia's face was pale and gaunt, but no fear was evident in it. Her long nun's habit suited her height.

"My dear," Blanca said, "I'll make you a cup of coffee."

They had studied together as far back as elementary school, but during all those long years they had never conversed as friends. Perhaps it was because Celia had been born Christian and wore a small wooden cross around her neck. Celia sat in the armchair where Blanca's mother-in-law usually sat. Blanca was about to say, *Why don't you sit in the armchair opposite? It's more comfortable.* But she realized that was foolish. A quiet glow burned in Celia's wide, dark eyes. She was evidently at peace with herself and had no need for any unnecessary gestures.

"How's your father?" Blanca asked.

"I just saw him. Everyone is picking on him, and I'm afraid for his health."

"He drew me up out of a deep pit," Blanca said, removing the scarf from her head.

Then Celia said, "Martin Buber's anthology has precious elixirs in it. When I was younger, I was sure that the Jews had no true faith. Grandpa used to say, 'In the church, there's music, and in the synagogue, people sweat.'"

"Are the stories about the Ba'al Shem Tov also about the faith of the Jews?" Blanca asked.

"Yes, so Martin Buber says."

"And do you think their faith is beautiful?"

"Very much so."

"Strange."

"What's strange?"

"After all, we're Christians, aren't we?"

"Contradictions don't put me off," said Celia.

Only now did Blanca sense how shallow her thinking had grown. In high school, under the tutelage of her teachers Weiss and Klein, the world had seemed like a work in progress that was striving to improve, to become clearer, more comprehensive, either plumbing the depths of the soul or ascending to the realm of the gods.

"What's become of me?" Blanca asked herself out loud. "I'm no longer what I was."

"I don't understand," Celia said.

"He says I inherited the faults of my mother and father, and Grandma Carole's craziness."

"And how do you answer him?"

"What can I say?"

Blanca walked Celia to the station. Celia spoke with longing about their distant and forgotten ancestors and about how much Buber's anthologies had helped her understand them. For only in Stillstein had she come to fully realize that her Jewish forebears, who were originally from Bukovina and had moved to Himmelburg at the end of the last century, were truly the flesh of her flesh. They were devoted people who worshipped God in simplicity, and if it hadn't been for certain disasters, their children would be worshipping God with the same simplicity.

"Are we still connected to them?" Blanca asked.

Blanca hadn't understood her friend's words, but she sensed that Celia, who had by now been living in the distant mountains of Stillstein for a year, had seen visions that had entirely changed her way of thinking. She was now connected with her ancestors, with nothing separating her.

"Take me with you, Celia." The words tumbled from Blanca's mouth.

"Don't be afraid. We're not alone. We have good and faithful ancestors who always dwell within us."

Blanca raised her eyes, and a chill raced down her spine.

30

ON FEBRUARY 16, 1908, after a long and difficult labor, a son was born to Blanca. At first she wanted to call him Erwin, after her missing father, but Adolf refused. He agreed to the name Otto, after her mother's brother, who had died young, in the middle of his university studies. Dr. Nussbaum extended her stay in the hospital, and Blanca nursed the infant morning, noon, and night, until she became weak from lack of sleep and, under doctor's orders, stopped nursing. Adolf heard about it and was angry, but he made no comment. She had noticed: in the hospital he controlled himself and didn't raise his voice. Dr. Nussbaum's efforts to restore the hospital to full capacity had failed. Just two wards were occupied. The others were deserted. Day and night, patients pounded on the doors, but he was unable to help them. The maintenance staff refused to work, and, lacking help, Dr. Nussbaum put on overalls and went to clean the toilets and add coal to the boilers to heat water for the laundry. The patients, most of them aged, complained a lot about their pains, about their children who had abandoned them, and about their old age. Dr. Nussbaum loved those old people. He went from bed to bed to examine them, and to tell a joke and make them laugh. Some of the old people spoke Yiddish, and Dr. Nussbaum, to make them happy, told them that he was born in the provinces, in a small town called Zhadova. His family had spoken Yiddish at home, and he was still fond of the language. The old folks forgot their age and their pains for the moment, and they told him what weighed on their hearts. Dr. Nussbaum listened and said, "May God have mercy," and that of course made them laugh heartily.

Blanca slept most of the day, but when she opened her eyes and saw Christina, the will to live returned to her, and she wanted to get to her feet and approach the window. Christina was devoted to her patients, never leaving them day or night. Sometimes, in the middle of the night, when a patient burst into tears, Christina would immediately rush to his bed, give him something to drink, and calm him down. Now that the staff numbered only two, she never took off her uniform. *If I possessed a love of humanity like Christina's,* Blanca thought, *I wouldn't have married; I would, instead, have worked in the public hospital. But I was weak, given over to myself and my own happiness.*

Adolf and his two sisters visited her. After that noisy visit, it was hard for Blanca to keep her eyes open. Drowsiness enveloped her like a blanket, and as she felt herself succumbing to it, she remembered exactly what Adolf's sisters had said to her and how they had looked at her. A great scream, like the sound of a falling tree, rose up out of her throat.

Christina held her hand.

"Now you look better," she said.

My life is shattered to splinters, Blanca wanted to say, *and it can be repaired only by labor and devotion. Otto will belong to his father, and I'll go to work in a hospital or an old age home.*

Later Dr. Nussbaum came and sat beside her. Now he was not only a physician. He was the hospital, in the figure of a single person. The pharmacist refused to provide medicines on credit, so Dr. Nussbaum paid him out of his own pocket. He took the trash down to the inner courtyard. When Blanca saw Dr. Nussbaum at work, she overcame her drowsiness and opened her eyes, marveling at every step he took.

"How do you feel, my dear?" he asked, leaning over her.

Blanca wanted to tell him that she felt a strong dizziness that pulled her down, that her legs were cold, and that she was afraid of the abyss yawning beneath her. She wanted to tell him, but didn't dare. She knew that Dr. Nussbaum's responsibilities were even greater now and that everyone was pressuring him. Dr. Nussbaum looked at her face and knew that Blanca lay in darkness, that she had to be watched over lest she do something desperate.

Sometimes, in the afternoon, when the heaviest drowsiness loosened its hold on her, Blanca felt a strong connection to her father and mother and to the country from which they had emigrated. It seemed to her that the Prut—in whose clear waters her mother and father and their forebears had bathed—was a purifying river, and if she ever managed to get to it, she would be saved from this stifling melancholy.

Thus the days passed. From time to time Adolf or one of his sisters would appear like a thick shadow. Blanca barely recognized them. One evening Adolf's elder sister came to visit her and asked, "When are you coming home?" Blanca tried to open her eyes. When they were open, to her joy she saw Dr. Nussbaum. "You don't have to answer," he said. She was immediately relieved and felt as though he had hidden her under the hem of his clothing.

31

BLANCA BEGAN TO feel better; she saw Otto and took pleasure in him. The other patients gathered around her, and they all said the baby was amazingly beautiful, that it had been a long time since they'd seen such a lovely baby. Dr. Nussbaum knew about Blanca's situation and said, "You'll stay here for the time being."

March was warm, and Blanca felt the closeness of her mother and father, and remembered the row of walnut trees that led to the high school. Sometimes she had met her teachers Klein and Weiss there, and they would talk on the steps of the building. The image was bright, as though time had transparently embalmed it.

Now her heart told her that she must go to Grandma Carole and reconcile with her. The last time Blanca had seen her, Grandma Carole was standing silently, her neck stretched upward, the sun's rays covering her dark face. She had looked like a statue that had been mummified for years, frozen in time. In her dream, Blanca had wanted to approach her and say, *Grandma Carole, don't you remember me?* But her legs wouldn't carry her.

When she awakened, Blanca heard a voice in the treatment room. First it had sounded like Theresa from the old age home, but it turned out that her ears had deceived her. It was her mother-in-law. She had come to take the baby to church so the priest would bless him.

"The weather is still chilly, and the child is weak," Christina explained to her.

"That's exactly why I came to take him. He needs a blessing to grow strong."

"But he's very weak."

"The cold won't hurt him. I raised five children, and all of them, thank God, are healthy and strong. The cold just strengthens them. And the blessing before baptism is a good charm for weak children."

"I can't give you the baby, only the doctor can."

"I'm the baby's grandmother, and I knew exactly what he needs."

Dr. Nussbaum arrived at a run and declared on the spot that the child was weak and must not be removed from the hospital.

The mother-in-law's jaw dropped. "Why?" she asked.

"Because he's weak."

"I'm taking him to the church. The priest's blessing will strengthen him."

"All of that must wait until he's healthy."

"I don't understand a thing," she said, and headed for the exit.

As she was leaving, Blanca's mother-in-law met one of her friends, and she complained to her that Jewish doctors had taken over the public hospitals, and they had neither loving-kindness nor mercy in their hearts. They took no account of the priests' opinions.

"Cursed be the Jews and their behavior." She didn't restrain herself now and slammed the door.

The next day, Adolf's sisters arrived and gathered in the corridor. They asked Christina whether the baby was still weak, why he was so weak, and whether there was any danger that he might be handicapped. They then asked permission to take him to the church. Christina explained once again what she had already explained. Hearing her words, the eldest sister said, "If he lies here all the time, he'll turn into a slug instead of a man."

Later, the sisters returned with a big, strong woman from a nearby village. They sat her on a chair and gave her the baby to nurse. Blanca saw the woman, her huge, dark breast, and the nipple that she stuffed into the baby's mouth. The baby suckled greedily until he choked. Everyone rushed to turn him over and pat him on the back.

When the baby was finished nursing, Adolf's eldest sister gave a banknote to the wet nurse. She took the bill in her dark hand, stuffed it into her coat pocket, and without saying a word headed for the exit.

32

BLANCA GREW STRONGER, and she would give the baby to the large woman who came to nurse him every day. First it seemed that the baby was gaining strength, but after a week of steady nursing, he began to vomit severely. There was no choice but to go back to the porridge that Christina had been carefully making for him. Blanca's mother-in-law wasn't pleased by the sudden change, and she kept saying that if the mother was weak, then the baby would also show signs of weakness. "In our family, thank God, everyone is healthy and strong."

Celia came to visit Blanca, who was so happy to see her that she started crying. Ever since Celia had brought her Buber's anthology, the book never left her hands. Even in her days of severe illness, she read it.

All of Celia's movements were familiar to Blanca, even the tilt of her neck, but she still wasn't the Celia she had once been. The Stillstein Mountains had changed her through and through. Celia spoke about her distant ancestors like someone who knew what she was talking about. She pronounced the names of their villages in Galicia and Bukovina as if she had just come back from visiting them the day before.

"You haven't shown Otto to me," said Celia. "How is he doing?"

Christina brought him in, and Celia said, "He looks like a darling baby."

"My husband and mother-in-law aren't pleased by his development."

"Blanca, my dear, we mustn't consider other people's opinions. You have to go your own way."

"If only I knew the way," replied Blanca.

The hospital's situation deteriorated. Dr. Nussbaum was working day and night. He grew so tired that he would collapse on a couch in his office in the middle of the day and fall asleep. The rich people who had promised to support the institution reneged on their promises. Dr. Nussbaum had already sent seven memorandums to the Ministry of Health, and what the municipality sent wasn't enough even for medicines. In his soul, Dr. Nussbaum knew that he would have no alternative but to send his patients home and close the gates of the institution, but he kept postponing the closure. His voice had changed over the past few days. He walked through the corridor with vigorous steps, shouting, "The rich have luxurious and roomy hospitals, and a well-trained medical staff. But what will become of the public hospitals? What will the poor and oppressed people do? Where will they go?" His speech was frightening, because he spoke to the bare walls.

The thought that one day Blanca would journey to the famous Carpathian Mountains and bathe in the Prut River took shape within her while she was ill, and now it was very clear. She imagined her life in the Carpathians as a simple life, a country life, with hours of prayer that would divide the day into three sections. On holidays everyone would put on white clothes and go to pray in small wooden synagogues. The disciples of the Ba'al Shem Tov's disciples still prayed in those small synagogues. They had reached a ripe old age and dozed during most of the day. But in the summer, in the drowsy hours of the afternoon, they sat in the doorways of the houses of study and greeted those who arrived with a blessing.

Blanca was sorry that her mother had told her so little about her childhood in the Carpathians. Her family had left the mountains when she was five, but she had retained some images of it in her heart. Blanca's father, on the other hand, had harbored resentment against his parents because of their poverty and because they had made it impossible for him to study at the university, and so for him everything there had sunk into an abyss.

"Thank you, Celia."

"What are you thanking me for?"

"For the anthology by Martin Buber."

Upon hearing Martin Buber's name, Celia inclined her head, as she undoubtedly did in the convent in Stillstein.

33

AT THE END of that week the gates of the hospital were closed, and Blanca started for home. She knew that strewn in every corner would be beer bottles and butcher's waxed paper in which sausages had been wrapped, and that the kitchen sink would be full of dishes. She knew, but even so, she didn't feel miserable that morning. The sun shone warmly, and Otto made her happy with every one of his gestures. In My Corner she was greeted with cheers. They served her coffee and poppy seed cake, and everyone made a fuss over Otto and agreed that he looked like Blanca.

When she got home, Blanca found the house as she had imagined it. She began at once to wash the dishes, pick up the papers, and empty the ashtrays. Otto fell asleep, and Blanca kept going to his bed to watch him as he slept.

After cleaning the house, she took Otto to her breast and then they went back to town to buy food for dinner. It was eleven o'clock, and Blanca hurried to return home. Near the butcher's shop, she looked up and to her surprise saw Grandma Carole. This time her grandmother wasn't standing and shouting; she was just sitting on the steps of the closed synagogue, curled up in a corner. Without thinking, Blanca rushed to the gate.

"Hello, Grandma Carole," she said. "I'm Blanca. Do you remember me?"

"Who?" she said, startled.

"Your granddaughter, Blanca."

"What do you want from me?"

"I wanted to tell you that I had a son, and his name is Otto."

"Who are you?"

"Blanca."

"What are you talking about?"

"Grandma."

"What?"

"Don't you remember me?"

Her sightless eyes began to blink nervously.

"What do you want from me?" she said.

"I wanted to beg your pardon."

"What are you talking about?"

"I'm Blanca, your daughter Ida's girl."

"Don't bother me," Grandma Carole said, and she made a gesture of rejection with her right hand. Blanca recognized that gesture and recoiled.

Blanca knew that Grandma Carole wasn't rebuffing her in anger. Her memory had faded, and she simply didn't remember Blanca any longer, just as she had probably forgotten her two other granddaughters who now lived in faraway Leipzig. But she was still angry.

When Adolf came home, he said, "You've come back, I see." It was evident that he wanted to say more, but the essence was conveyed in that sentence.

"I feel better," Blanca said. For a moment they both looked at Otto while he slept. He was relaxed, and his face, lit by the sun, seemed content.

Blanca rushed to serve Adolf his dinner, and while doing so she told him that Dr. Nussbaum was in despair. The wealthy people who had said they would provide assistance hadn't kept their promise.

"Why are you telling me all this?" he asked without raising his head.

"What will the poor people do who need help? Whom will they go to? To whom will they turn?"

"Who told them to be poor?"

Blanca fell silent. She was familiar with those coarse pronouncements of his, but now they scraped her flesh with an iron brush.

After dinner, Adolf went to the tavern and Blanca remained where she was. The long day had left her hollow. It took her a while to find the words within her. *Adolf hates me,* she said to herself, *because I'm thin and weak, and because my parents were Jews. Apparently my conversion to Christianity changed nothing. And now I'm even thinner. I weigh less than one hundred and ten pounds. What must I do in order to change? I have to eat more and work in the garden, but I'm very weak, and it's hard for me to stand on my feet.*

Adolf returned from the tavern very late.

"Where are you?" he shouted from the doorway. Blanca, awakened by his loud voice, hurried over to him and helped him over to the bed. He immediately fell down onto it, and Blanca took off his shoes and covered him with a blanket.

That Sunday Otto's baptism ceremony was held, and everyone wore festive clothes. After the baptism, the priest spoke about love and compassion, and to Blanca it seemed that he was talking to Adolf, asking him to behave like a Christian toward her. The little church was full of people and the fragrance of incense. Blanca made a great effort to remain on her feet, but toward the end of the ceremony she stumbled. Adolf picked her up and reprimanded her for not being careful.

"I'm sorry," Blanca said, standing up again. Then her mother-in-law passed Otto back to her, and Blanca looked at him and hugged him to her breast.

After the ceremony they served strong drinks and honey cake to the guests. Some girls from school, whom Blanca barely remembered, approached her and hugged her. Adolf looked content in the company of his friends, who surrounded him and congratulated him. He was especially happy with his cronies from work, who looked like him, suntanned and strong.

Now Blanca remembered the bar mitzvah celebrations in the synagogue. Her mother used to take her to them now and then. It was crowded there, too, but most of the people were short, and their presence wasn't crushing. She and her mother would stand together and watch everyone celebrating. At the end, they would go up to the bar mitzvah boy, congratulate him, and depart. Public places and crowds of people had made Blanca sad since her childhood. Her mother knew that and would bring her to these ceremonies only occasionally. Now she had to learn how to cope with that, too.

"How do you feel?" Adolf's eldest sister asked her.

"Fine," said Blanca, glad she had said so.

34

THEN CAME LONG, hot days, and Blanca worked in the garden early every morning. The neglected garden bloomed again. On rainy days she tidied the house, did laundry, and decorated Otto's cradle. When Otto woke up at night, she got out of bed, fed him, and sang to him. Adolf wasn't pleased by these nightly attentions. "Let him cry," he said. "The devil won't take him." But Blanca wasn't at ease with this approach. She would go over to Otto's cradle and rock it. Once Adolf commented, "He'll turn into a slug." Blanca noticed that his sentences, like his movements, were abrupt; he explained little, and what he said cut like a razor blade.

The good thoughts that had made her throb with life in the hospital died out on their own, and again she became what she had been: a maidservant, working from dawn till dark and crushed under Adolf's heavy body at night.

Dr. Nussbaum tried with all his power to raise money to reopen the hospital, but his efforts were in vain. Having no choice, he turned his home into a hospital. Dozens of people crowded the gate of his courtyard and sought his aid. Whatever he could, he gave.

One day, the doctor met Blanca downtown and invited her to join him for a cup of coffee in My Corner. Blanca was embarrassed to admit to him that Adolf treated her the way he did and, also, that he kept grumbling, "Jewish doctors won't tell me how to behave." Dr. Nussbaum looked into her eyes and knew what was on her mind.

"You have to come to see me every month," he said. "And if your husband abuses you—tell me immediately."

After that she thought of going to Himmelburg, but she put off the trip. She was afraid to travel with Otto. Adolf would have said,

"He's weak. He's pale. With us, children aren't like that." Blanca used to bring the cradle out into the garden so he'd get some sun. To her dismay, this only brought out his delicate features, and she stopped. One night in a dream she saw her father standing in the courtyard of the old age home, as though he were trapped. His face was gaunt, and an unfamiliar expression of irony, not his, flickered in his eyes.

"Papa!" she called out, and awoke.

The next day she gathered her strength, diapered Otto, prepared food, and set out. At the old age home, Theresa hurried over to her and cried, "Here's Blanca!" and everyone was excited.

"The child looks a lot like you," Theresa said. "What's his name? Otto? A nice name. His features are very delicate. Let's pray that fortune favors him." They sat in the kitchen and drank coffee, and Blanca knew that her life had no attachment to any place now. Theresa wasn't a delicate woman; she was straightforward and understanding. You didn't have to explain to her what harm a cruel husband did. She had felt it on her own flesh.

"The situation here couldn't be worse," Theresa told Blanca. "The treasury is empty, and the Jews of Himmelburg are no longer as generous as before. Conversions are many, and the children deny their parents. They do send us some money from Vienna, but it isn't enough for regular maintenance."

"So what are you going to do?" Blanca asked anxiously.

"I don't know. I simply don't know."

"Doesn't the church help?"

"Have you forgotten, dear, that this is a Jewish home?"

Theresa mentioned the old age home in Blumenthal again, and all the advantages Blanca would have if she worked there.

"You have to be far out of his reach," she said. "Every hour that a woman saves herself from a beating is a pure benefit."

"What should I say to him?"

"Tell him that you want to work and contribute to the livelihood of the house."

"And who will watch over Otto?"

"A housekeeper. I raised three children that way."

"I'm so afraid of the beatings, and now I'm afraid he'll hit Otto."

"You mustn't be fearful, my dear."

"I tremble all the time."

One of the old people approached her and said, "We sometimes remember your father here. He was a very special man. We all liked him. Since he abandoned us, we've missed his great soul. You know that Jewish saying, don't you?"

"No."

"It's a marvelous expression. It's more than an expression."

Blanca didn't know how to respond, so she said, "This is my son, Otto. He's growing and developing nicely."

Theresa continued to speak about children who neglected their parents, and about old age, with its diseases and torments. If it weren't for God, whom we believe in and cleave to, she said, were it not for the strong feeling that He is close to us, our lives would be a horror.

"Blanca, my dear, it seems to me that the Jews have lost their connection with God, and that makes their lives so much harder."

"Do you stay in touch with your children?" Blanca asked.

"If they need money, they write to me."

"And who comes to visit you?"

"Only my sister. She lives very far from here, but she always comes, and she brings me things. She knit this sweater with her own hands."

"Strange," said Blanca.

"Why do you say that it's strange? That's how it always was, and that's how it always will be." Her face displayed a frightening honesty, as though the years had engraved every injustice and distortion on it. Anyone who looked at her knew that life was flooded with sorrow and filled with clouds.

35

THE MONTHS PASSED. Otto was already crawling, and Blanca reconciled herself to her painful body and clouded life. Sometimes she would remember earlier times, and they seemed hidden to her, as though they were part of the life of another woman. Even the town, where she knew every corner, now seemed to belong to the church.

Every Sunday she went to mass. The family made a point of attending on Sundays and holidays. There Adolf was also surrounded by friends, embracing them, chatting with them, laughing. Blanca never missed confession. She would kneel and say, "I didn't want to see my mother's death, and I fled from the house. Afterward I abandoned my father in the cemetery. I'm a sinner and worthy of death." The priest listened and asked no questions.

Once, however, he commented, "Our Lord Jesus has already atoned."

"But my sin is unbearable."

"Pray. Prayer will drive away your bad thoughts."

"It's hard for me to pray, Father."

Sundays were the hardest day of the week: in the morning in church and afterward, the gathering in her house. Those parties brought together many of Adolf's friends as well as his relatives, and they became merrier and dizzier from week to week. Blanca would serve the guests and chat with her mother-in-law. Her mother-in-law had suffered a lot in her life, but she didn't complain.

"Man is born to labor," she would repeat, "and let him make no reproaches to his fellow." It was clear that this saying wasn't hers. Still, it sounded as if it was.

Adolf knew no mercy now, either. For every mistake or forgetfulness she would pay, but sometimes he would also hit her for no reason, the way you beat an animal.

"You're not a woman," he would say. "You're a monster. You're like your father, like your grandma."

"Don't hit me," she would beg, but that only increased his anger. In the end she would lie on the floor, absorbing the blows without reacting.

If it weren't for Otto, for the look in his round eyes, she would have gone to the river and leaped into the water. But Otto would rescue her and draw her out of despair. He would wake up, open his eyes, and call out, "Mama," and immediately all the clouds scattered and fled.

More than once, after a night of searing pain, Blanca was about to say, *I want to go out to work and help support the household. All the women work, and I want to work, too.* But she was afraid to say it, lest Adolf agree. Otto was now her life and her support. She took him everywhere with her. When she worked in the kitchen, she placed the cradle next to her, and when she worked in the garden, she would take the cradle outside. Blanca spoke to him and told him stories, and when he laughed, she laughed with him.

Adolf was completely given over to his comrades. Over the past few months his face had grown fleshier and had become flushed, like the face of a drunkard. He resembled his father more and more: the same drunken look, the same arrogance. He spent most of his wages in the tavern, and he gave Blanca only a few coins, over which he also got angry. Blanca was frugal, and she made their meals with everything that the garden produced. Sometimes she couldn't afford milk. Her body bled and hurt, but she was afraid to say, *I'm going out to work.* Once, the pain was so great that she said, "You're driving me out of this world."

"What are you talking about?" he said, and headed out the door, as though she were nothing but a ghost.

In the end, it was Adolf himself who declared, "You have to go out to work."

"How?" She was stunned.

"All the women work. My mother works, too."

"And who'll take care of Otto?"

"We'll bring a woman in from the country."

At first she deluded herself into believing that it was just a passing thought, but when he kept pressing her, she understood that he wouldn't let up. A new fear possessed her. *I'll run away,* she said to herself, but she knew she didn't have the strength to go far: Adolf's huge hand would reach her. Once he said to her, "I never miss a thing. I know all your intrigues."

The next morning, after Adolf went to work, she prepared some sandwiches, dressed Otto, and they set out for Blumenthal. The old age home in Blumenthal was different from the one in Himmelburg. The building was spacious, and around it was a well-tended garden. The director of the place asked for information about Blanca's life, and she told her.

"And who will take care of your child?"

"A country woman."

"We're very strict here about lateness and absence."

"I'm orderly."

"So, you'll start in a week, on Tuesday at eleven o'clock. I'm writing it in my journal."

When Adolf came home from work, she announced to him that she had found a temporary job in the old age home in Blumenthal. Without looking her in the eye, he said, "Fine. We have to find a woman from the country." Later he asked when she would be starting her job, and Blanca told him.

It was a week of rain, fear, and great weakness. At night she begged, "Don't press so hard on me. I can't breathe." Those pleas just increased his fury. But for some reason he didn't hit her. Toward the end of the week she said, "Otto, I'm going out to work. I have no choice. What can I do?"

Blanca washed, ironed, and prepared clothing and bedding. The dread she felt at the thought of being forced to part from Otto in a few days clung to her body like a cloak of fire. Again she saw her mother's prolonged, slow death. During the last months of her life, her mother had struggled to get up every morning and tidy the house. Her father would try to help her, but his assistance wasn't effective. Her mother would say, "Erwin, why don't you sit down and tell me something."

"What should I tell you?"

"What you want to tell me."

She tried to be especially pleasant to him, to renew the old hopes, and she managed to do so. Blanca's father was elevated by his wife's optimistic mood, and he began to make plans again. Her mother knew in her heart that the plans would lead to nothing, but she listened to everything he said. She knew that in a little while he wouldn't have an attentive ear. In the last months of her life, her love had been soft and merciful. At the time, Blanca hadn't grasped the wonder of it. Now it was as if the light of their faces shone again.

36

ON MONDAY ADOLF brought home a tall, strong woman from the country and said, "This is Kirtzl. Show her what to do in the house."

"I'll show her everything," Blanca said in the tones of a maid-servant, and went right out into the garden.

"This is the vegetable garden," she said. "In this season there are eggplants, squash, and also cabbage." Blanca looked at the woman closely: her face was full and flat, and a heavy smile hung on her lips.

"Do you water the garden?" Kirtzl asked stolidly.

"In weeks when there's no rain."

They passed on into the kitchen, and Blanca said, "There's wood in the shed."

"You don't use charcoal?" Kirtzl asked in the same tone of voice.

"No," Blanca said, and the word reverberated in her head for a moment.

Then they went into the bedroom, and Blanca said, "This is Otto. He's not an infant anymore. He sleeps through the night, eats well, and he's developing nicely. Do you know how to take care of children?"

"I have three."

"How old are they, if I may ask?"

Kirtzl smiled. "They're already in school," she said.

"Do you want to have a cup of coffee, perhaps?"

"I wouldn't object."

Adolf went out with his friends, and the two women sat and

talked. Kirtzl told Blanca that her husband had run off six years earlier, and his trail was cold. The children had been little, and she raised them.

"Didn't the police look for him?"

"Go look for a needle in a haystack."

"I also have to go to work." Something of the woman's voice clung to Blanca.

"Don't worry. I'll watch out for your husband and son. You can rely on me."

Blanca's former life seemed like a dream to her: she had been a free person, she had parents who loved her, she was excelling in high school, she read books, and in the afternoons she would sit with her father in My Corner. And then, because of a grave sin that she had committed, she became a prisoner. Until now she had been in this prison, and tomorrow she would be transferred to another one.

Kirtzl seemed to comprehend her thoughts and said, "I don't complain."

"No?"

"I've learned to grab whatever comes my way," she said, pursing her lips.

"How?"

"Don't you understand?"

"I," Blanca said, "never leave the house."

"If so, this will only do you good."

Blanca felt that this sturdy woman had a lot of strength, but she couldn't tell what kind it was. At any rate, she noticed: Kirtzl had sat down on the chair slowly, and when she was sitting there, her body filled it.

"Where have you been working until now?" Blanca asked.

"In the village."

"Weren't you happy there?"

"The men molested me," she said, and her smile revealed her large teeth.

"Here things will be quiet for you," Blanca said distractedly. Then she ran out of words. "Kirtzl," she said.

"What?"

"It's hard for me to part from Otto."

"Don't be emotional," Kirtzl said. "It isn't good to be emotional. Life is rotten."

Blanca couldn't sleep that night. Evil visions horrified her, and she sat in the dark kitchen, awaiting the morning. The night was long, and she knew clearly that without Otto, her life would be even more abject. The statue of the crucified Jesus that hung above the altar in the church appeared before her. But for some reason his face was strong and angry.

Before going to work, Adolf reminded her that she had to come home on Saturday afternoon to prepare the house for Sunday. Blanca was groggy, but still she ironed his shirts and arranged the cupboards. Finally she fell to her knees and begged Otto not to cry.

Kirtzl arrived at eight, and Blanca rushed out to catch the morning train. On the way, she met a former classmate. Andi was a simple, reliable girl whom Blanca had thought about now and then. Now, when she met her, she could say only, "Excuse me, I'm running to catch a train."

Andi, astonished by her sudden appearance, called loudly after her, "God preserve you."

Blanca got to the station at the last minute, bought a ticket right away, and boarded the train. The buffet car was empty, and she ordered a brandy. During her pregnancy and for some time afterward, Blanca hadn't drunk. Now she felt a strong thirst for a drink. The first shot of brandy blurred her, and she saw the statue of Jesus again. His face had changed once again: now it didn't seem angry, but determined, as if he were about to detach himself from the nails and take revenge against his tormenters.

Then her head emptied. The blur thickened, and a dull pain took hold of her scalp, spreading across her temples and down to the nape of her neck.

"Do you have a damp cloth?" she asked the waitress who was serving in the buffet. "My head is splitting with pain."

The waitress handed her a cloth.

"Here," she said softly. "This will make you feel better."

Hearing her soft words, Blanca burst into tears.

"What's the matter, dear?"

"I left my son behind, and I miss him."

"I understand you very well. I also left my two little girls behind and went out to work."

"How can you stand it?"

"It's very hard for me. Every day I dull my longing with cognac. It's been three years now."

The damp cloth made Blanca feel better, and she sank into a pressured, choking sleep, but in the midst of it she heard a clear voice.

"Blanca, you mustn't despair. There is a God in heaven, and He watches over you. You have to do what God tells you to do. Your suffering is not in vain. Your life has a purpose." It was Theresa's voice, coming from a distance; not a soft voice, but a very endearing one in its simplicity. Blanca opened her eyes. The train was close to Blumenthal. She pulled herself together and rose to her feet.

37

BLANCA QUICKLY LEARNED how different the old age home in Blumenthal was from the one in Himmelburg. In Blumenthal there were regular times for rising in the morning and for lights-out, the meals were served on time, there was a rest period from two to four in the afternoon, and visitors were permitted only on Tuesdays. The director of the home was strict with the residents, and if they disobeyed her instructions, she scolded them out loud and sometimes punished them.

Upon arriving, Blanca was sent to clean the rooms and make the beds. Then she went down to help in the kitchen. In the kitchen she met Sonia and quickly made friends with her. Sonia had been born in Sarajevo. Her mother was Jewish and her father was Croatian. From her childhood, Sonia had been attracted to Jews. Her father wasn't pleased by that inclination, but Sonia was so enchanted by Jewish people that at an early age she left her home in order to live among them.

"What attracts you to the Jews?" Blanca asked her.

"I don't know. My mother never talked with me about being Jewish, but I've been interested in them since my girlhood. I would stand for hours next to the synagogue and listen to the prayers. Are you Jewish?"

"I was," said Blanca, embarrassed by the direct question.

"Why did you convert?"

"I got married," said Blanca, without explaining.

In the evening the director summoned Blanca to her office and explained the conditions of service.

"You work for six days," she said, "and you go home on Saturday afternoon. Anyone who is absent without an excuse or is negligent will be fired on the spot. You'll share a room with Sonia, and there will be a special announcement regarding night shifts. By the way, my name is Elsa Stahl, and you may call me Elsa." Her look was blue and cold, and it was evident that she was a strict woman who wouldn't hesitate to punish.

Sonia was three years older than Blanca. She had finished high school in Serbia and begun to study to be a pharmacist, but she had lost interest in her studies and abandoned them. Since then she had been wandering. She'd already been to Vienna, and now she was here, saving money so she could travel to Galicia.

"What attracts you to Galicia?"

"The old-time Jews."

When Sonia spoke about the old-time Jews, her eyes widened and a spark gleamed in them.

"When I was in the hospital," Blanca said, "my friend brought me a book of stories about the Ba'al Shem Tov."

"I never heard of him," said Sonia.

"It's a book about the Jewish faith."

"Marvelous!" Sonia cried.

Sonia was an enthusiastic woman, bold and extravagant. She didn't hide her thoughts. The residents liked her, but the director was suspicious of her. Once she had proclaimed to one of the janitors, "What difference does it make that my mother is Jewish? I'm proud of it."

"You mustn't talk that way," one of the residents commented.

"Why not?"

"Because being Jewish isn't something to be proud of."

"But I am proud," said Sonia.

After a few days of depression and humiliation, Blanca felt her strength returning to her, and sensations throbbed within her once again.

"I've been married for more than two years, and I have a son named Otto," Blanca told Sonia.

"And your husband?"

"He works in the district dairy."

Sonia told her about the old age home and its residents, and about Elsa, who treated the old people cruelly. The old people were afraid to complain. Every time a delegation came from Vienna to check on the conditions of the old age homes in the provinces and they asked the old people about the place, they answered as one: everything is fine, everything is decent.

Blanca still didn't understand everything that was being told to her. She still was overcome with fatigue.

"I don't know what's the matter with me anymore," she said, as she fell asleep.

In the middle of the night Blanca awoke, terrified.

"What's the matter?" Sonia asked.

"I'm frightened."

"Of what?"

"I saw Otto near a deep pit, and I couldn't save him."

38

FROM THEN ON, Otto never faded from Blanca's view. She heard his voice in every corner, and on every floor she saw him crawling to her.

After a few days of fear, Blanca was about to return home, but at the last minute she changed her mind. She knew that Adolf would make a sour face and say, "Why did you come back?"

At night Sonia would sit on Blanca's bed and tell her about her childhood and youth. While she was studying in high school, she had been a communist, and her boyfriend was also a communist. The two of them were going to go to Switzerland. But once, as though in passing, her boyfriend said to her that the Jews stood in the way of redemption because they were petits bourgeois in their souls and that the revolution was hateful to them. At first she didn't catch the meaning of his words, but once she did, she understood that old-style anti-Semitism was coming from his mouth. That very week she broke off her connection with him and with the party.

Were it not for her nightmares, Blanca would have been immersed in the hard work. But they would return each night and bring Otto with them. Now Otto looked like baby Jesus lying on a pile of straw. The yellowish colors surrounding him looked unpleasant.

"Otto!" she would cry, alarmed. Hearing her voice, he would

move a little, but he wouldn't respond, as though he had been kidnapped and wrapped up like a mummy.

Blanca slept very little, so as not to see Otto in the figure of Jesus. She sat in the kitchen, and if one of the residents was hungry or couldn't sleep, she would sneak a sandwich to him.

Elsa lived outside the old age home, but she had informers—two janitors who flattered her and told her what was happening in the home at night. Luckily for the other workers, the janitors were sound asleep after midnight, and not even shouts could awaken them.

Sonia also told Blanca about her father, a wise, sensitive man who had studied philology for two years but whose hatred of Jews was boundless. Every time he spoke about them, his rage would burn. When Sonia was little, her mother used to object to his prejudices, but in time she stopped. She had gotten used to his arguments and even believed them a little. Once Sonia had been very close to her parents, but over the years a barrier of alienation had arisen between them. Now all she wanted to do was get to Kolomyja, her mother's birthplace.

"What do you expect to find?"

"I don't know, but my heart tells me that I have to go there."

"I would very much like to join you, but I'm shackled."

When Blanca laid her head on the pillow, Otto came back, looking out at her from the long oil paintings that hung on the walls of the church. A cold, sad, puzzled expression appeared on his pure face, as though he were wondering, *What am I doing here, and what will my fate be when morning comes*? Dry plants and people bent over with hunger surrounded him on every side, but Otto was lost in his amazement and ignored their plots against him.

"Dear," Blanca whispered to him, "watch out for those people. They're plotting and liable to harm you."

Hearing her voice, his lips parted and he said, "Don't forget. I'm Jesus Christ, and no one can harm me."

"But you're also my son," Blanca said, alarmed.

"Correct, Mother, but no one knows that."

For a moment Blanca was happy, but when she woke up, her head was spinning, her heart was pounding, and she felt weakness in all her limbs. Only at noon, when she was serving lunch to the old people, did the feelings of oppression let up slightly. The old people liked her and told her about their sons and daughters who had converted to Christianity and who were ashamed to have parents living in a Jewish old age home. Among the residents there was an old storekeeper named Durchfall who didn't hold his tongue.

"I'm a Jew," he proclaimed, "and I'll never hide it. It's not a special virtue, but it's also not a shame. At Hanukkah we'll light candles and sing 'Rock of Ages,' and we'll remember the times when Jews were Jews and their Judaism was dear to them, when they were prepared to rise up against a mighty empire."

Sometimes Durchfall spoke in a different tone of voice.

"There's no doubt," he would say, "the Jews are a changeable and frivolous nation. It's hard for them to be Jewish, it oppresses them, and at every opportunity they throw a few old books into the Danube. They're sure that if they convert to Christianity, their neighbors will embrace them and take them to their hearts. They're wrong. They're simply wrong."

39

WHEN BLANCA RETURNED home on Saturday, she noticed from a distance that the front door was ajar and that the garbage pail kept it from closing. A faded November light shone on the empty lots around the house. She had come at a run from the station, but when she approached the house, she halted. The anxiety that had shackled her body for a week wrapped itself around her legs, and she felt her knees weaken.

At a distance from the door she called out loud, "Kirtzl!" No one answered.

"Kirtzl!" she called again, and for a moment she stood frozen, trying to absorb what was happening. She opened the door and went inside.

Kirtzl was sitting outside in the garden, wearing a loose cloak. Her stolid face conveyed a kind of indifference, the relaxed expression of an idle person.

"How are you?" Blanca addressed Kirtzl as though she weren't a woman sitting across from her but, rather, a large animal. Because you couldn't know how it would react, you quickly appeased it.

"What?" Kirtzl said, her mouth falling open.

"Where is Otto?"

"He's in his room," she replied, without moving.

Otto was standing in his cradle, wide-eyed. Blanca sank to her knees, extended her arms, and started to pick him up. Otto burst into tears, frightened by her sudden return.

"It's Mama," Blanca said, putting him down. "Don't you remember me?"

Kirtzl got up and stood very close behind her. Blanca felt her fullness and moved aside. Otto cried, and Blanca tried in vain to calm him. Kirtzl observed her desperate efforts without interfering, but eventually she said, "Give him to me." Blanca passed Otto to her, and, to her astonishment, he stopped crying.

"How did you do that?" Blanca asked distractedly.

"You have to lift him up high," Kirtzl said tonelessly.

It was two o'clock, and it seemed to Blanca that she had done her duty, that now she had to return to the old age home. A week of separation had distanced her from those oppressive rooms. Even Otto seemed different to her, perhaps because of the blue shirt he was wearing. He had received that shirt some time ago from Adolf's elder sister. The sister had said at the time, "That's a boatman's shirt. Anyone who wears a shirt like that will be as strong as a lion." Because of what she'd said, or maybe for another reason, Blanca had never touched the shirt, and it lay in the bottom drawer of the dresser. She had hoped that Otto would outgrow it and never wear it.

"Mama," Otto suddenly called out, as if he had just realized she was his mother, and reached out toward her. Blanca took him and held him to her heart. She immediately forgot she was working in the old age home in Blumenthal and far away from Otto. It seemed to her that she had been sunk in a long sleep and now she had awakened.

"How is Adolf?" she asked.

"He's fine," Kirtzl answered briefly.

Only a week had gone by since Blanca had departed for Blumenthal, and Kirtzl's fingerprints were in every corner. It wasn't the house she had left. Every piece of furniture appeared to have changed shape. To the smell of beer and tobacco the scent of cheap perfume was added. But she discovered the most conspicuous change of all on the wall: a blue icon, Jesus in his mother's arms.

"Who hung up that icon?" Blanca asked, feeling as though it were no longer her house.

"I did," Kirtzl said. "A house without icons is liable to meet disaster." Kirtzl spoke like a peasant.

Now Blanca noticed that Kirtzl wasn't as ugly as she had seemed to be at first. Her broad shoulders suited her face and her full, solid body. For a moment Blanca was about to ask her how one grows such a sturdy body, whether the sun did it or thick corn porridge, but then she realized that it would be a stupid question, and she kept her silence.

"Did Otto ask about me?"

"No."

"And did you change his diapers at night, too?"

"You don't change children's diapers at night."

"Why not?"

"They have to get strong."

Kirtzl had the confidence of a peasant who had received the lessons of life as an inheritance from her ancestors.

"And how was your work?" Kirtzl surprised her by asking.

"The old people are sweet."

"And they didn't make passes at you?"

"They're old people."

"There are old men with very young urges. In our village, there's an old codger who sleeps with his niece every night."

Blanca looked at her broad face again. A kind of satisfaction filled it. It was clear to Blanca that a head like that, stuck onto a sturdy neck and planted on cushioned shoulders, never got dizzy. She never vomited and she didn't have insomnia, and when she got up in the morning, guilt feelings didn't gnaw at her. Her limbs were fastened on well. She had no backaches and no weak knees.

"And are you pleased?" Blanca asked for some reason.

Kirtzl smiled a narrow, secret smile, which immediately revealed what had happened in the house during the week that Blanca wasn't there. After eating his dinner, Adolf had made clear how it was going to be and then left for the tavern. When he came back, he had gotten right into Kirtzl's bed, peeled off her nightgown, and, without any niceties, mounted her. Later, after nodding off for a while, he had mounted her again. Then she had become heated up and planted her teeth in his neck. Adolf had kneaded her and eaten her flesh with a greedy mouth. Toward morning, before leaving for work and while she was still groggy, he had mounted her again, gotten dressed, and gone out.

Blanca looked at Kirtzl and knew with certainty that this was what had happened. A secret jealousy flooded through her, as though she understood for the first time that there were healthy, coarse people for whom life was intended, and the rest were thrown to the side.

40

WHEN ADOLF CAME home from work, he pierced her with a look and asked, "How was it?"

"Fine," Blanca answered, matching his tone.

Adolf's face was flushed, and it was clear he had downed quite a few drinks, but he wasn't drunk. Repressed rage filled his face and traveled down the nape of his neck. Blanca rushed to serve him his meal—whatever was in the pantry and what she had managed to prepare. Adolf didn't complain. He sank into his plate and made no comment.

Blanca sat at some distance from him and observed him—the way he cut the steak, then sliced the bread and broke it into cubes. He dipped the cubes in the gravy and put them in his mouth. That was how his father ate, and so did he. But this time, for some reason, it seemed to her that with those movements he was imitating an unusually large dog that she had seen the night before in a dream and that she had been frightened of.

"How was it?" she asked after a prolonged silence.

"I worked." He dismissed her with brevity.

"And how was Kirtzl?" she had an urge to ask.

"Fine."

Blanca knew every detail of that abrupt way of speaking. Adolf had never had a real vocabulary, but the little that did emerge from his mouth was sufficient for him to express himself. Among his friends in the church and the tavern he spoke a lot, but in fact he used the same words over and over.

When Adolf finished the meal, he asked, "How much did they pay you?"

Blanca rose to her feet, picked up her purse, and took out the banknotes. With the same hand she took out the coins as well and laid them on the table.

"Not much," he said, not touching the money.

"That's what I received."

"They have to pay you more."

"That's the salary."

"The Jews are always exploiters."

It seemed to her that he was going to fold the banknotes, gather the coins up in his hand, and slip them into his pocket.

"I'll need money for fare on Monday," she dared to say.

"Very well," he said, and left a banknote on the table.

Blanca took the bill and put it into her purse.

"I'm going out," he said.

In the first weeks after their marriage, Blanca used to implore Adolf to stay. *Don't go out, don't leave me alone,* she would say. *Just for an hour or an hour and a half,* he would reply, *and I won't drink a lot.* She would sit at home and cry, and when he came back, she would pretend to be happy. Eventually she stopped asking. She understood that his cronies and the drinks were more important than she was. As long as he enjoyed her body, he didn't despise her, but after she became pregnant and started vomiting, his attitude changed: he stopped talking to her and his sentences shrank to just a word or two, as though she were no longer his wife but a beast of burden that had fallen ill and was no longer useful.

Now she stood to the side and observed the way he put on his coat, tightened his belt, opened the door, and, without saying another word, went on his way. Over the next hour he would sit with his buddies, drink, brag, and tell a coarse joke about his Jewish employer. Then he would pull the bills she had given him out of his pocket and pay for them all, proudly proclaiming, "Tonight the drinks are on me!" the way she'd heard him announce more than once. The thought pierced her for a moment. She planted her feet on the floor and didn't move. But the joy of having Otto in her arms, of being able to look into his eyes and talk with him, was so overwhelming that the way Adolf had robbed her a moment ago was erased from her mind.

That evening she had a few drinks and told Otto about her father and mother. She recalled the high school and the mathematics and Latin teachers, she spoke at length about Grandma Carole, and she said, "The work in the old age home in Blumenthal is exhausting and humiliating, but after darkness the light will come, and we will never be separated again." She spoke in a torrent, mixing past and present, and she was so tired that she sank down on the floor next to Otto's cradle and fell asleep.

Adolf apparently came back very late. He shouted and cursed, but Blanca didn't hear him. Still, something apparently filtered into her sleep, because she was frightened and got up. When she opened her eyes, Adolf was already lying on the bed with his legs stretched out like the drunks who used to sprawl in the square not far from the high school.

The next morning, Blanca rose early, dressed Otto in clean clothes, and immediately left for church. She didn't wake Adolf because he had once said to her, "Don't you ever dare wake me!"

In church she met her father-in-law and mother-in-law and Adolf's sisters. They all asked how Otto was and made a fuss about his hair; it went without saying that they didn't ask how his working mother was. They were concerned only about the crown prince.

After mass the family and some guests came to the house. Adolf was merry and greeted them with hugs. Blanca rushed to serve sandwiches and drinks. Every step was hard for her, but she made an effort and stayed on her feet.

"Blanca, let me tell you something: you shouldn't serve sandwiches without pickles," her mother-in-law commented.

"I didn't manage to pickle any cucumbers this week."

"I prepare them in the summer, so that I'll have a supply in the winter."

"In the future I'll see to that," she said, to avoid quarreling, but her mother-in-law wasn't content with that apology and went on to say, "You have a big garden, and you can grow all your vegetables in it."

"I was working in the old age home in Blumenthal this week," she said, trying to defend herself.

"I also worked away from home when I was young, but I never neglected the house. The house comes before everything else. That's our temple, and we must watch over it like hawks."

Now Blanca felt the anger that had been repressed within her since her return. It flowed through her arms and extended to her fingertips. She was alarmed. She hugged Otto and said in a quavering voice, "I understand." Her mother-in-law apparently sensed the repressed anger and fixed her with a venomous look.

41

THUS THE WEEKS sped by, and the seasons changed. Every Sunday Otto would break Blanca's heart with his weeping. In the first weeks, he seemed to be getting used to her absence, but that was only how it appeared. His cries for help grew steadily stronger, and she could hear them in distant Blumenthal.

One Monday, while Blanca was running to the station, Brandstock, the storekeeper, stopped her and told her that Grandma Carole had died the previous night. The funeral party was leaving from her house at noon. Then he turned and walked away.

"What?" Blanca gasped.

Brandstock was one of the few people in town, perhaps the only one, who was still an observant Jew. He was a short man with an unpleasant look. He would sometimes appear in her father's store, buy something, and then announce out loud that the merchandise there was more expensive than in another store, but that he, Brandstock, was committed to buying from Jews and would always do so. Her father, of course, would get angry at that remark and retort, "You aren't obliged to." To which Brandstock would respond, "I'll never change. This is how I've always acted, and this is how I always will in the future."

Blanca, plagued with guilt feelings because she had left Otto behind, didn't absorb Brandstock's bitter message at first, but when it did register she started running toward the granaries that stood along the Schenau River to catch up with him and get more details.

But, as though in spite, Brandstock had disappeared, as if the earth had swallowed him.

"I have to go right away," she said, and turned toward the railway station. After she had gone some distance, she realized that she was walking in the wrong direction and turned around. It was eight thirty, and thick, foggy clouds crept over the houses. Only the tower of the municipal building and the trapezoidal roof of the school stood out.

Grandma Carole's house was not far away from there, but ever since her marriage Blanca had avoided the house, and it had faded from her memory. It was a house of the kind that was no longer built, made of wooden beams. In the past people used to daub special oil on the walls, making them shine and last a long time, but in recent years they had stopped oiling the walls, and they were turning gray.

"I must go straight," she said, and started walking. It was not the way to Grandma Carole's house, but the way to the high school. For a moment she was glad to be walking on that path again. Not until she reached the Kumers' store did she realize that she had made a mistake and that she would be better off heading for the center of town, to find out what had happened and to prepare for what was to come.

In My Corner people already knew about Grandma Carole's death, and they came up to Blanca and hugged her. There was no one in town who hadn't encountered her, and there was no convert to Christianity who hadn't been wounded by her tongue. Nevertheless, they harbored respect for her. Everybody knew she was an honest, courageous woman and that Judaism was more important to her than her body.

One of the storekeepers, whose name Blanca didn't remember, said, "Carole was a great and brave Jewish woman. It's too bad we didn't know how to appreciate her when she was alive."

"Now you're saying that?" A voice was heard from the back of the room.

"I always said it."

"I never heard it."

The voices surrounded Blanca on every side, and they moved her. The owner of My Corner refused to accept payment for her coffee and apologized because he wouldn't be able to attend the funeral. Blanca was embarrassed and confused.

"You have to take this from me," she said. "It's your livelihood."

Whereupon the proprietor answered emotionally, "You're like a daughter to me. I won't accept it."

When Blanca reached Grandma Carole's house, the door was already open wide. In the living room, where Blanca used to play on the floor for hours when she was a child, Grandma Carole lay covered in a white sheet. Two candles burned near her head. The members of the Himmelburg burial society had already performed the necessary tasks, and they now stood at some distance from the deceased woman, waiting for mourners. "My name is Blanca, and I'm the dead woman's granddaughter," she said, introducing herself.

"Aside from you, are there other relatives?" asked a member of the burial society, without any special courtesy.

"There are two other grandchildren, but they live in Leipzig."

"Out of respect for the deceased, we need some details."

"I'm prepared to help in every way," Blanca said, and immediately felt that her words were out of place.

"What was Grandma Carole's Jewish name?"

"I don't know, sir, on my honor, I don't know. We called her Grandma Carole."

"And what were the names of her father and mother?"

"I don't know that, either."

"Was your grandmother observant?"

"She was very meticulous in matters of the tradition, Rabbi."

"I'm not a rabbi," said the man.

"Sorry."

"How or from what did the deceased pass away?"

"I don't know, sir. For the past two years, I haven't spoken with her."

"Why?"

"She was angry at me, sir. I married a Christian and converted. Grandma Carole never forgave me for that. Once I tried to ask forgiveness from her, but she wouldn't forgive me."

"I understand," said the man, bowing his head.

"And what will we do now, sir?"

"We'll wait for the prayer quorum."

Blanca knew that her question was stupid, and she was embarrassed. The winter light streamed through the windows and scattered the shadows that had gathered in the corners. Blanca remembered now that when she was a girl, she and her mother used to come here and sit on the sofa. Then, too, a sudden light would pour in and illuminate the dark corners.

Meanwhile, Brandstock arrived and said, "I didn't manage to get anyone to come. People don't want to come to a Jewish funeral. What can I do?"

"I don't understand," said the head of the burial society.

"That's how it is with us, sir. The children become apostates, and their parents deny the tradition of their ancestors. What can I do?" There was no grace either in his look or his expression. His face betrayed the bluntness of a practical man, not a reader of books, and his manner of speech came from his store.

"We brought five men from Himmelburg, and a woman to ritually clean the body, and you can't get together that number of people in this town?"

"I admit it: it's a scandal, but I can't do it. It's not in my power. I went to all the Jewish stores and announced the funeral to them."

"And what did they say to you?"

"They nodded their heads."

"And no one promised to come?"

"Not a single one. You have to know, sir, that the deceased woman was hard. Every day she would stand at the entrance to the synagogue and denounce the converts to Christianity. They didn't like her in the town, and it's no wonder that nobody is coming to her funeral."

"Strange," said the head of the burial society, and he went outside.

Later, a few old men and women gathered and stood around the dead woman. One of the old men complained about their having left her on the floor. The head of the burial society explained the reason for that to the old man, but the old man wouldn't agree with him and argued that a Christian burial was dignified. They didn't leave the corpse on the floor. The Jews had contempt for their dead.

Then the funeral procession left for the cemetery. The old men apologized and said, "We can't walk that far," and they went home. The men from the burial society bore the coffin, followed by Brandstock, the woman who had cleansed the body, and Blanca. The woman who had cleansed the body uttered broken syllables along the way. They sounded like suppressed complaints. She sighed and finally kept silent. Blanca staggered after them, surprised that everyone else was walking with robust steps and she alone was trailing behind.

The cemetery was empty, and its open gate showed that it had been days since anyone had visited it. Seeing the neglect, Brandstock raised his voice and said, "The Jews also neglect the cemetery, and they won't be forgiven for that in the world of truth. In the world of truth, there's no favoritism. They'll all be punished, believe me."

The men from the burial society didn't listen to him but started to dig the grave right away. Blanca observed the men who were digging. They weren't the same men who had arranged her mother's funeral. They were younger. Their faces expressed effort and concentration, and it was evident that they were doing their work faithfully.

After the grave was dug and the coffin was placed in it, the men from the burial society began to recite prayers. They prayed loudly, emphasizing the words. After the prayers, Blanca approached them and thanked them.

"There's no need to thank us," said the head of the burial society.

Blanca then left the cemetery hurriedly so she could catch the noon train. She ran with determination and reached the station within a few minutes. In the buffet car she had two drinks and sat next to the window. Now, with clarity, she saw the morning's chain of events.

Kirtzl had appeared at eight o'clock, and Blanca had handed Otto to her. Otto had refused to part with her and shouted, "Mama, Mama!" Blanca had sat down and said, "Dear, I'm not going far. I'll come back very soon. Don't worry." Her voice seemed to soothe him, and he stopped crying. Afterward she had slipped out of the house without saying good-bye to him. At first she had stood at the door and listened. Not hearing the sound of crying, she had set out, but after taking a few steps she heard crying again and was about to go back. Then, out of the fog, Brandstock had appeared and told her the sad news.

"Otto!" she said out loud, downing another glass of spirits. "Your mother just saw Grandma Carole to her final rest. Grandma Carole was a woman of principle, and she wounded me more than once, but I can't be angry with her now. Unlike me, she was loyal to the faith of her ancestors and defended it with her body. I wanted to tell you that, so that no secret will divide us. Now you have to know everything, and indeed I will tell you everything. You will be with me wherever I go, my dear." Hardly had the words left her mouth when dizziness took hold of her head and shook her. Blanca put her hands over her face and leaned against the wall of the train. She had almost arrived at Blumenthal when she realized that it was already five o'clock, and Elsa would certainly be furious. Anxiety drew her out of the dizziness, and she grasped the railing and stepped down cautiously from the train.

42

BLANCA REACHED THE old age home in Blumenthal at six o'clock. It was already dark. Elsa stood at the entrance to the corridor, and when she saw Blanca, she thundered, "I don't want to see you here!"

Blanca just stood there, motionless. "Grandma Carole died, and there was no one to attend her funeral. Forgive me."

"And who will take care of these people?" Elsa pointed to the inmates lying in the rooms.

"What could I do?" Blanca replied, her arms upraised.

"You could have come here on time." Elsa continued to hammer at her.

One of the veteran workers dared to approach Elsa and said, "Forgive her."

"How can I forgive her?" Elsa addressed the woman angrily.

"Blanca is devoted to the old people, and she doesn't avoid any task."

"She was late by six full hours. That's an unforgivable sin," Elsa said, and went into her office, leaving Blanca standing outside. Two women who lived in the home and had witnessed the unpleasant scene entered the office and said, "Forgive her."

That last request was apparently effective. Elsa came out and announced, "This time I'm forgiving you, but I won't do it again. From now on, you're on probation."

Blanca went back to work. She prepared the tables for supper and served meals to the bedridden residents. This was her home now, and she was glad to be in the company of the old people. Some of them were tall and thin, and imbued with an old-fashioned nobility. They observed more than they spoke, with the sharpness of people who had lived fully in the world for many years and seen what they'd seen. Their expressions were clear, quiet, and merciful. In contrast to them were the irritable ones who never stopped complaining about the sons and daughters who had converted and abandoned them. Day and night they rummaged through everything that had happened to them during their lives, casting blame and raising the ghosts of long-departed men and women. Everyone at the home knew everything about them. Because they talked about it so much, their pain was discolored, and all one saw was bitterness and misery.

Blanca was glad to be working and helping people who needed her assistance, and the events of that long and painful day began to fade. One of the bedridden women asked her about Grandma Carole, and Blanca told her.

While the last meals were being served to the people in beds, Elsa burst into the dining room. This time she vented her fury on Fritz, the plumber. That tall, sturdy man didn't seem surprised. Without raising his head, he asked, "What's the matter?" The question heightened her rage. Fritz didn't respond. He just moved to the side, as though he had met up with a mad dog. Fritz was a lazy, drowsy man who did only what was necessary. Elsa had sworn more than once that she would fire him, but she hadn't carried out her intention. Fritz was strong, and he helped everyone. He picked sick people up in his arms and carried them to the infirmary or the toilet. He loaded onto his back furniture, valises, sacks of flour, and whatever else needed carrying. He was no longer young, but his strength had not waned. When Elsa would explode, he would stop what he was doing, and after she wore herself out with shouting, he would go back to his room, lie down on the bed, and doze off.

That night Blanca told Sonia about Grandma Carole's death. Sonia asked for details, and Blanca said simply, "Grandma Carole was not a woman of this world. It was hard to get near her, because she was like a pillar of fire."

"What do you mean, Blanca?" Sonia tried to understand.

"She defended the faith of her ancestors with her body."

"Did you ever speak with her?"

"I couldn't speak with her. How could I speak with her?"

"I've never met Jews like that."

Blanca noticed that Sonia's body didn't suit her face. Her body was sturdy like a peasant woman's, but her face was long and thin, and when she paid close attention to something, it appeared even narrower.

The conversation with Sonia unexpectedly clarified something for Blanca: her mother's religious beliefs. For years Blanca had been sure that her mother, like her father, was distant from her tribe and its beliefs. Only now did she grasp clearly that her mother had kept a hidden connection with the faith of her ancestors. She refrained from showing her feelings only because of her husband, whom she loved. Once, when Blanca's father was complaining about the store, about his partner, and about the debts into which he had sunk, her mother said, "There is a God in heaven, and He watches over all of His creatures." Upon hearing those words, her father buried his face in his hands.

"Where did you get that strange belief?" he asked.

"It's my faith," she said, without raising her voice.

"That was your ancestors' belief, not yours." Blanca's father tried to correct her.

"Mine, too, if I may."

Hearing her last words, Blanca's father raised his head and said, "I don't believe what I'm hearing."

Blanca's mother responded to that with a restrained smile, and the conversation ceased.

"Soon I'll be leaving Austria to the Austrians and traveling to the Carpathians," Sonia said.

"What will I do without you?"

"I'm sure you'll get there, too."

"I don't see how."

"I already see you there."

Thus the days passed. During breaks between shifts, Blanca would tell Otto what she was thinking. She was sure not only that Otto could hear her from afar, but also that he could understand her. Once one of the residents approached her and asked in surprise, "Blanca, are you praying? I didn't know you were so religious."

"I'm not praying. I was just mumbling something, apparently. Sorry."

There was an extremely aged woman named Tsirl in the home. Like Blanca's mother, she had been born in Zelishtshik and remembered Ida Beck's family and its ancestry, and she told Blanca that Ida was a descendant of the legendary Rabbi Nachman of Horodenka. Just the mention of his name brought blessings.

"I didn't know," said Blanca.

"It was no accident that my daughter hospitalized me in this place, and no accident that you came to work here. There is a reason for everything, my child."

"What was so special about that rabbi?"

"He wasn't a rabbi, dear. He was Rabbi Nachman of Horodenka."

"Do you remember Grandma Carole?"

"Certainly I remember her. She was many years younger than I."

"She passed away yesterday."

"May her memory be blessed. In the world of truth, they will receive her well," she said, and closed her eyes.

Tsirl dozed most of the day, but when she opened her eyes, her gaze was clear and she remembered everything very well.

The next day she told Blanca, "It's hard for me to die in a foreign place. If I were in Zelishtshik, I would have been gathered to my ancestors long ago. This alien place is delaying death, and a person lives a long life for no purpose."

43

THE WINTER WAS long and harsh, and Blanca would return home leaden and dejected. Kirtzl had taken over the house. The cheap perfume that she used filled the rooms and smothered them. On every wall she had hung an icon. It was clear: Kirtzl was no longer Blanca's helper; she did Adolf's bidding. With every passing week, Otto was more and more neglected. His rear end was chapped, and an unpleasant odor wafted from him.

It was now Kirtzl's house, not Blanca's. Sometimes Kirtzl would ask her, "How is it there?" to emphasize that Blanca belonged to the old age home in Blumenthal and not to this house. Blanca suffered but didn't complain. In Otto's company she was full of joy and contentment. She would wash him and rub his sores with salve, and then she would sit with him and show him the big letters in the children's book she had received as a gift from one of the residents of the home. When Otto would cry, Blanca would promise that the day was not far off when she would no longer go out to work.

Adolf's behavior became more brutal. In the past, when he took her wages he would leave her with money for the train fare and a little pocket change. Now he gave her only her train fare, and he would always say the same thing: "They're exploiting you and not paying you properly."

"What can I do?" She would stand before him as though paralyzed.

"Demand more."

Otto would awaken at night and burst into tears, and Blanca

would rush over to soothe him. One Sunday she secretly brought him to Dr. Nussbaum. Dr. Nussbaum quickly determined that the child was neglected. Blanca told him she was working away from home and saw Otto only on weekends.

Dr. Nussbaum had changed a lot since Blanca last saw him. The battle he was waging against the municipality and against the health authorities in Vienna had left its mark on his face. His fingers trembled. There was now some hope that the gates of the hospital would soon be opened, but not all its departments. Meanwhile he continued treating patients in his home and courtyard, and if he was summoned at night, he didn't refuse.

"How is Celia?" Blanca asked.

"She's in seclusion. That is her path now. What can I do?" When he spoke about his daughter, the physician's authority evaporated from his face.

The Sunday parties continued as usual. Blanca would do the cooking on Saturday night, rise early for church, and then quickly prepare herself to receive guests. She was anxious because her in-laws spoke about Otto as a weak-bodied child, doubting that he would be able to meet the demands of life. To strengthen him Blanca fed him chopped liver that she brought from the old age home.

"Otto must be strong," she said. "Here you have to be strong. You have to eat a lot and stand powerfully on your own two feet. Grandpa Erwin and Grandma Ida would have taken care of you differently, but they're no longer with us. What can I do? Don't cry. People who cry are weak. And you're not weak. You're as strong as a lion cub, and no one will dare to touch you."

Adolf would return home late at night half drunk and shout, "Why's he crying? Shut him up!" His threatening voice was very frightening, and Otto would quiet down. Adolf would then collapse on the bed and fall asleep.

Blanca's anxieties no longer gave her rest. She worked many night shifts, and in return Elsa would free her for a few hours during the day. She would rush to catch the noon train and come back by the evening train. Once Adolf caught her and said, "What are you doing here in the middle of the week?"

"I came to see Otto."

"What for?"

Otto's features, as though in spite, became more delicate. A quiet intelligence glowed in his eyes. It was as if he understood that the people surrounding him were putting him to a hard test. When Blanca appeared, he would stretch out his arms, hug her around the neck, and cling to her. Blanca kept promising him that his suffering would not last long, that soon they would set out on a long journey. In the few hours that she was with him every week, she taught him new words. Otto would look at her lips and try to imitate the sounds.

Parting from Otto on Monday mornings was agonizing. If it weren't for the two shots of brandy that Blanca had in the buffet car, the pain would have been constant. But by the time she returned to the old age home, the pain, roused from its slumber, would torture her again. Finally, though, her work wiped that pain away, too. After a day of labor, she would lay her head on the pillow, her thoughts scattered to the winds.

Meanwhile, Sonia also got into trouble. One of the janitors informed on her for making soup for two old people in the middle of the night. Sonia confessed, and Elsa decided to adopt a new method of punishment: to deduct from her wages. Sonia responded with fury and threatened to complain to the old age home's board of trustees. Upon hearing her threats, Elsa dismissed her on the spot.

The residents repeatedly asked Elsa to forgive her, but Elsa stuck to her guns.

"If everybody in the old age home does whatever he feels like," she said, "anarchy will reign here, not order." "Order"—that was the ideal for whose sake she tormented both the workers and the residents. She never tired of proclaiming, "There will be order here. This is not some Jewish market."

True, the old age home didn't look Jewish from close up. The old people didn't sit in the lobby or in front of the entrance to the building. Flowers and houseplants were placed in every corner. In that matter, as in others, there were disagreements among the residents. Some of them claimed that Elsa had turned the place into a grim Protestant temple, or into a prison where they punished old people for being old. Others argued that strict discipline was better than Jewish commotion. Elsa was strong in her resolve to dismiss Sonia, but in the end, because of the residents' pleas, she forgave her. She informed her that from now on she was working there on probation. Any infraction, even a small one, would result in her immediate dismissal. Elsa used to punish the residents in similar fashion. For example, anyone who didn't dress neatly or who neglected to tidy the area around his bed wasn't taken on the weekly excursion to the river.

"We're Jews, not Germans," one of the residents stated, daring to raise his voice.

"Order is the honor of life," replied Elsa. "Without order, there is no honor. Jews are negligent about order and discipline, and that's to their discredit."

"To hell with discipline."

"Not here."

Despite everything, there were little pleasures. When the tale-bearing janitors were soundly asleep, Blanca and Sonia would take out the pot of compote and serve anyone who was hungry.

44

THUS PASSED THE WINTER. In the spring Sonia got into another fight with Elsa and she was fired, just as Elsa had threatened. Sonia stuck to her guns and didn't mince words.

"This isn't a home for people," she said, "it's a prison. I'm going to walk through the streets of Blumenthal and tell everyone that there's a jail in the middle of their city where they torture old people." Before she left, she addressed the residents.

"People are born in the image of God," she said, "and they have to preserve His image." She was about to say more, but the two janitors took hold of her and dragged her outside. Even after she was outside, she didn't hold her tongue.

"A jailer, not a woman!" she shouted. "That's what she is."

In the evening Blanca sneaked out to the Lilac Café, where she used to sit between shifts. Sonia was waiting for her. It was the Sonia she knew so well, but somehow different. A storm raged in her eyes, and every gesture throbbed with anger. Sonia told Blanca that she intended to leave for Galicia on the very next train. She spoke about Galicia with fervor, like someone speaking about his beloved native city.

They sipped brandy and drank coffee, and Sonia talked about outer freedom and inner freedom, and about the obligation to destroy institutions like Elsa's old age home, to set the tormented old people free. Blanca was alarmed. Sonia's face was firm with the resolve of believers who had removed all fear from their hearts. Blanca tried to get her to delay her departure, but Sonia said that Austria was a prison and that she must reach Kolomyja as soon as possible to purify herself from this contamination.

They sat for a while in silence, and then Blanca saw Sonia to the railroad station. The station was dark and enveloped in a damp fog. The train soon arrived, and Sonia said, "Blanca, you also have to free yourself from the bonds that they put on your hands and feet, and go forth from bondage to freedom, to the place where your ancestors worshipped God." Fire burned in her face, but her words were serene, rising from a tranquil heart. The train rushed away, and for quite a while Blanca stood where she was in silence. It was hard for her to drag her feet back to the old age home and start the long night shift.

Now the days proceeded heavily, as though stuck in heavy batter. Week after week Blanca would take the train home, sometimes two or three times a week. The nights became a journey of longing for freedom, but with no way out. Kirtzl entrenched herself in the house. Her limbs broadened, and an animal-like satisfaction filled her face. When Blanca asked her why Otto's skin was so chapped, she answered, "You worry too much. I raised three children, and they're alive and healthy. Your worries won't bring him health."

Adolf would grab Blanca's wages from her hands and ignore her. She noticed that he also ignored Otto, as though he were a bastard and not his son. Otto grew taller, but his body didn't fill out. His scrawniness was evident in his exposed ribs and in his face, which became long and thin.

"He has no appetite," said Kirtzl.

Sometimes in church Adolf would remember Blanca's presence and stand next to her. In the flat shoes she wore now, she came to just below his shoulder. If he wanted to crush her, he could do it with one shove.

Why am I so frightened? she kept asking herself. She drank more and more. Drinking filled her with waves of warmth, but not with words. *How strange,* she thought as she spoke to Sonia in her mind.

There are no words in my mouth. Once I knew how to talk, how to express things in detail and with precision, but now, when I stand next to Adolf, my tongue cleaves to the roof of my mouth and I can't think of a single sentence with which to answer him.

A change was also taking place in her body. She had already observed that now, when she picked up heavy things, the burden didn't hurt her. And during that imaginary conversation with Sonia she noticed something else: an arm motion, a reaching upward that didn't seem to come from within her own body, a gesture that Grandma Carole used to make while she stood at the entrance to the synagogue.

Blanca said to Otto, "Don't be afraid. I'll watch over you with all my soul and all my might." Hearing her voice, Otto opened his eyes wide and laughed, but Blanca was dejected, and in her dejection she began to sob.

On the train one Monday morning Blanca had a few drinks, and she returned to the old age home in a blur. Elsa smelled it on her right away.

"What you do outside isn't my business," she said, "but you can't come here reeking of alcohol. I don't intend to reprimand you again."

"I'll try," Blanca replied in the tones of a maidservant.

"I'm not talking about trying," said Elsa.

Now, too, Blanca felt the muteness that blocked her mouth. She rushed to her room, changed clothes, and without delay went to clean the stairs.

The alcohol that Blanca had drunk in the buffet car seeped into her and strengthened her. After cleaning the stairs, she made the beds and mopped the floor. She did all the chores without thinking, and at the end of the day she reported to the dining room and brought trays to those who were eating. The strength of youth, such as she had not even felt in high school, flowed in her arms. One of the old people observed her and said, "What's happened to you, Blanca?"

"Nothing. Why are you asking, sir?"

"You look different today."

She soon learned how right the man was. On laundry day she found a diamond ring in one of the smocks. In the past, whenever she had found anything valuable, she quickly returned it to its owner. This time she looked at the ring for a moment and then slipped it into her pocket. After finishing the laundry she thrust the ring into a cleft in the wall.

The theft seemed to have passed unnoticed. But then two weeks later, Mrs. Hubermann discovered that her ring had disappeared, and she burst into tears. All the old people demanded that a worker named Paulina be fired, because stolen jewelry had already been found in her possession. Paulina was summoned to Elsa's office, and she swore by everything dear to her that she hadn't stolen a thing. But her oath didn't help her this time, and she was dismissed. Before leaving, she cursed the residence and the Jews who had plotted against her. The two janitors took hold of her the way they had gripped Sonia and threw her out.

From then on Blanca stole money and jewels, quickly slipping them into her hiding place. Sometimes at night she would go downstairs and fondle them. "I'm not stealing for myself, but for Otto," she murmured like a slave woman. Contact with the stolen jewels restored to her a moment of joy.

45

BLANCA'S LIFE WAS now submerged in a rigid, impermeable schedule. Shadows clung to all her steps. Once she saw two gendarmes at the entrance of the old age home, and she was sure they had come to arrest her. She was also afraid of the janitors, and of bringing compote to the old people at night. Since Sonia's departure, Blanca was apprehensive about breaking any of Elsa's rules. In the past she had sat with the old people, helped them, and stolen food for them. Now she did her duty and departed. A feeling of uncleanliness, similar to what she had felt after her marriage to Adolf, stained her again. She bathed immediately upon finishing a shift, but the feeling didn't fade away.

Elsa grumbled and threatened to bring the police to make a search and interrogate the staff. Aside from Paulina, who had been fired, there was another worker who had once been caught stealing cheese, and suspicion was now directed at her. No one knew what Elsa would do. After her shift, Blanca would flee to her room and curl up under the blanket.

On the weekends Blanca would return home and surrender her wages to Adolf. Then she would rush to bathe Otto and dress him. Blanca tried to do in one day what a mother does in a week: she washed his clothes, took care of him, and amused him, and on Monday morning she bathed him again and hurried to the railway station. Because of a change in the schedule, there were no more night trains, and so Blanca was no longer able to return home for a few hours during the week. On Saturdays they let her leave at eleven, and she saw Otto by the late afternoon.

So the summer passed. In the autumn Otto began to cough a lot, and Blanca brought syrup for him from Blumenthal, but the cough didn't go away. When she wanted to take him to Dr. Nussbaum, Adolf commented, "You're going to doctors again."

"Otto's coughing a lot."

"We all cough, and nobody dies."

Blanca spirited Otto out to Dr. Nussbaum. He examined Otto and determined that the cough was serious and that if it wasn't treated, he was liable to catch pneumonia. Blanca raced straight to the church from the doctor's office. After the service, a lot of guests came to the house, and she served them sandwiches and drinks. Eventually they all dispersed, and Blanca remained with Otto.

"Mama," Otto called out clearly.

"What, dear?"

"Sit next to me."

"I'm sitting."

"Don't go away."

"I'm not going away."

"I'm afraid."

"Of what, dear?"

"Do you have anything nice to give me?"

"I have pudding."

"Don't go away."

"I'm not going."

Blanca sat and looked at him. A golden light poured onto his face, and he looked like the baby Jesus in the long painting above the altar in church. His face was pure, and his lips were closed tightly in concentration.

"Otto." The word slipped out of her mouth.

"What, Mama?"

"Nothing."

Just then the sun went down, and shadows were cast on the walls. Blanca hid her face in her hands, as she had done in her childhood when the fear of death assailed her.

46

A WINTER WITHOUT snow blew over the vacant lots near the old age home. The janitors were busy chopping wood most of the day, and their tight faces grew darker. Aside from their work in the courtyard, they did Elsa's other bidding: they informed on the other workers and on the residents. But Elsa still didn't trust them fully, either, and she punished them more than once. The janitors took it in stride. "Life isn't worth a penny," they would declare.

Several times Blanca was about to go down to the laundry, remove the jewels from their hiding place, and free herself from the nightmare. In her sleep she saw herself dragged off in handcuffs. Since Sonia had left for the east, Blanca's life had no horizon or words. She worked from morning till night and was afraid of every shadow.

Sometimes, in the railway station, Blanca would meet a friend from high school or an acquaintance from the past. Those brief encounters left scratches on her heart. On her last trip she had met a friend from elementary school, a girl from a simple family who hadn't excelled in anything and who also stuttered. The boys used to pick on her, and she would crouch in the hallway and cry. It was a muted, broken sobbing that sounded like a stifled whimper.

"Mina!" Blanca called out. She ran to her and hugged her. Mina hadn't changed much. Her face was narrow, and her lips trembled a little. Now, too, speech cost her much effort.

"Surely you're continuing your studies," said Mina.

"No."

"But you did so well."

"I got married."

"The teachers were so proud of you, and they always used you as an example."

"They were exaggerating."

"In my eyes you were a symbol of perfection," said Mina, hanging her head.

They sat in the station café, and Blanca told her that since her wedding she hadn't opened a book. She was working in the old age home in Blumenthal, and a woman from the country was taking care of her son.

At the end of the winter, Otto came down with a high fever, and Blanca took him to Dr. Nussbaum. Dr. Nussbaum examined him and directed her to have him hospitalized immediately, so Blanca went to Blumenthal to ask Elsa for leave without pay. To Blanca's surprise, Elsa was generous this time and authorized her leave without saying a word. She even wished Otto a full recovery. Blanca was so moved that she stood up and said, "Thank God that good and generous people help me." Then she went to take leave of the old people. They also rose to the occasion, collecting a tidy sum and including some dried fruit and a box of candy. Blanca was so embarrassed she could only say, "I can't find words to thank you." Then she left. In the buffet car on the train she drank two brandies and fell asleep. She dreamed that she heard Mina saying, "Nothing can help us, sister, unless we overcome our muteness. Muteness is what paralyzes us."

Otto was burning with fever, and from day to day his condition worsened. Dr. Nussbaum didn't leave his bedside, and at night Blanca would sleep next to him and dampen his lips. In her nightmares she saw her mother sitting in a wicker armchair. She was young and was wearing a poplin dress. That was how Blanca would sometimes find her when she came home from school. Blanca usually brought good news, and her mother would say with restraint, "If only the good angels would stay at your side." It was as though she were suspicious of happiness. At the time Blanca wondered why her mother couldn't just be happy. Now her meaning had become clear to Blanca: all those years ago she had been anxious about her daughter's fate.

47

THE FEVER WEAKENED Otto, and his face was as pale as chalk. Dr. Nussbaum didn't conceal his opinion: "For the moment, he mustn't be removed from the hospital and you must be at his side, watching over him."

"And what about my job?"

"They'll have to extend your leave. I'll give you a medical certificate."

Blanca set out for Blumenthal right away to ask Elsa for additional leave. At that cold, clear afternoon hour the tranquillity of the winter's end wafted from the low neighboring houses. She remembered that time of day from years gone by, and the memory seared her.

When Blanca reached Blumenthal and asked for an extension of her leave, Elsa's face soured and she said, "We can't extend your leave, and the choice is up to you."

"Please, show mercy."

"Mercy isn't the issue. It's order."

"I'm lost," Blanca whispered to herself.

Elsa rose from her seat and said, "Don't pity yourself too much. No one owes you anything. You chose what you chose. We have to suffer in silence without making a fuss."

Good God, Blanca said to herself. *There's some justice in her meanness.*

Blanca went to her room to pack her clothes. The room was in darkness and still full of Sonia's presence, as if she had left behind some of her essence. It was palpable, spread over the table and the two chairs.

What should I do now? she asked herself.

You have to go downstairs and take the jewels. Blanca heard Sonia's voice, plainspoken and without a trace of sanctimony. Blanca was fearful, and Sonia spoke again. *You have to go downstairs without hesitation. Otto's life is more important than the Ten Commandments.*

Blanca knelt and bowed her head. She felt for the first time that she was in the hands of forces more powerful than she was. Then she went downstairs to the laundry room. The darkness struck her in the face, but she easily found the hiding place. She shoved the jewels into her coat pocket and went upstairs to say good-bye to the old people.

Finally she went over to Tsirl. Tsirl put her hands on Blanca's head and blessed her. Blanca didn't understand a word of what she whispered. After the blessing, Blanca kissed her hands and walked to the door.

Tsirl stopped her. "Where are you going, dear?"

"My son is very sick, and I'm going to him."

"You have nothing to worry about, daughter. You have good protectors above, and God who cures the Jews will also cure your son. What is his name?"

"Otto."

"The good Lord will watch over all the Jews and over him."

Blanca didn't move. The wings of the blessing hovered over her, and afterward, too, on her way to the train, she still felt the soft touch of the words. But later, when she was close to Heimland and felt the weight of the jewels in her pocket, she got up and stood next to the window, exactly the way her late father had done when all hope was lost and despair had gripped him.

When Adolf heard that Blanca had been dismissed, he seethed with rage and slapped her face. Blanca burst into tears. Her weeping inflamed his fury, and he heaped words on her: "Just not to work, just to sit in the house, just to feed your weakness."

"I'll keep working," she said, trying to mollify him, but it didn't work. He stamped his feet.

Blanca worked in the hospital now. On Sundays she would come home, hand her wages over to Adolf, and prepare refreshments for the guests. Her mother-in-law, who came to visit Otto, said, "Otto's sick again. What will be with him? There's something out of order in him. He's sick all the time."

Blanca looked her right in the eyes and said, "Dr. Nussbaum says he'll be a sturdy young man."

"Let's hope so. But I can't see it. Doctors always make promises and never keep them. By the way, Blanca, you should change your name. A name like yours is an obstacle."

"Father Daniel already gave me a name."

"When?"

"After the baptism."

"So why don't you use it?"

"It's strange to change your given name."

"What's strange about it? If the name is harmful, you have to change it. In two or three years Otto will be going to school. Everyone will know right away that his mother's name is Blanca. You don't have to display your defects. By the way, what name did Father Daniel give you?"

"Hilda."

"A nice old name. In the village where I was born, that was a common name."

Otto was very weak and barely opened his eyes. Dr. Nussbaum came to see him several times a day. Blanca didn't move from his bedside. Now she remembered her mother and said to Otto, "If you swallow the pill, you'll feel a lot better. There's nothing easier than swallowing a pill." Those soft words rang in her ears with pure clarity.

Meanwhile, Celia returned from the mountains. Her face was round and transparent, and filled with wonder. Her simple nun's habit made her look taller. She spoke softly and listened intently. Sometimes she asked a question.

"I'm bound in fetters, and I don't have the strength to loosen them," Blanca said to her.

"What do you mean, Blanca?"

"I'm living in a prison, and I stopped counting the days that I've been in captivity. Every day closes in on me more. I had a good friend in Blumenthal, but she went to the east. I would gladly have gone to the Carpathians, but I'm married and I have a child."

Celia's eyes widened, but she said nothing.

"I can tell you that ever since Grandma Carole died, I've felt a strong attraction for the Carpathians. Maybe the mountains will give my soul back to me. I feel that the soul within me has fled."

"And you wouldn't want to come with me to the mountains of Stillstein?"

"Churches don't love me," Blanca replied.

After parting from Celia, Blanca sat in the hospital corridor, and to her surprise she felt that a hint of strength still fluttered within her. She rose to her feet and approached Otto's bed. His sleep was quiet now. That night he felt better, and the next day he opened his eyes.

48

ONLY NOW DID Blanca see how much the malady had changed Otto. He had grown taller. His face glowed, and the words in his mouth were clearer.

"The disease has passed," Blanca told him, "and in a little while we'll go home."

"I want to be with you."

"I'll always be with you," she said and kissed his forehead.

Otto knew more than she imagined. He knew, for example, that the job in Blumenthal had been exhausting and that Elsa had mistreated her, that Kirtzl wasn't his aunt, that Grandma and Grandpa came every Sunday, drank cognac, and grumbled. He'd evidently taken in a lot during his few years. Blanca was astonished by the abundance of words he'd collected.

"I'm afraid of Kirtzl," he told her.

"Why?"

"She walks around the house without any clothes on."

"She's apparently used to that." Blanca tried to distract him.

Otto's recovery breathed a new energy into Blanca. She was hungry and ate whatever was served, and at night she sat and talked with Christina. Her life, which had seemed as though poised on the edge of a steep slope, now seemed to have been given a reprieve. An old, youthful strength coursed through her legs. In her heart she knew that hard days were in store for her, but fear didn't deter her. At night, lying on the mat next to Otto's bed, she would wander off to faraway lands with him, sailing on boats and struggling through flowing currents.

Blanca didn't imagine how close at hand the solution was.

Before she left the hospital, Dr. Nussbaum told her, "Otto has recovered, but he needs to be watched over. Don't put him in the care of that peasant woman. If there's any need for my intervention, notify me right away."

"I don't know how to thank you."

"You have to be a brave woman."

"I promise," Blanca said, and she was glad that those words had emerged clearly from her mouth.

When Blanca returned home she found Kirtzl sitting in the armchair, dressed in a housecoat. Her full face had gotten even fuller. *Your job is over,* she wanted to say. *You have to go back to your village, and I'll stay with Otto. Otto is recovering, and I have to watch over his recovery.*

Kirtzl seemed to guess her thoughts. She rose to her feet, and with a peasant's cunning she said, "Welcome. Otto, why don't you say hello to me?"

"Hello."

"Is that all?"

Blanca didn't know what to say and sat down. The confidence she had felt earlier evaporated. Once again iron walls surrounded her, stifling her into muteness. *Dear God,* she said to herself, *I went to grade school and after that to the municipal high school. Why can't I say a single sentence?*

"Are you going back to work?" Kirtzl asked after a silent pause.

"No. They fired me."

"And what do you plan to do?"

"I don't know."

"Are you looking for another job?"

"I'm not looking. I don't have to look," said Blanca, and her fingers trembled. Kirtzl apparently sensed her anger. She turned around, went into the bedroom to get dressed, and when she came back out she said, "I'm going home. The food for Adolf is ready in the pantry. I'll come back next Monday."

The heavy smell of butter stood in the air. Blanca remembered that when she was in elementary school, the country girls used to spread butter on their hair. She had suffered from the smell but never complained about it.

When Adolf came home, he said, "You have to find work right away."

"I'll go and look," she replied, to avoid contradicting him.

"On Monday, first thing."

I have to suffer a little more, she said to herself, without knowing what she was saying. Only at night, in her sleep, did the meaning become a bit clearer. In her dream she saw Grandma Carole brandishing a long knife like a sword and calling out loud, "Arise, sleeping fathers, from your slumber, arise and save me from the apostates. I declare war and await you. Only with you can I defeat that great camp. Come, together let us break through the locked doors of the synagogue, so that the God of Israel will be revealed in all His splendor."

49

ON MONDAY BLANCA left the house. As she got ready to go, Otto wrapped himself around her legs, encircling her with his arms and not letting her move. Blanca promised him that this time she'd come back soon. At that, he let her go and said, "You promise, but you don't keep your promises."

"This time I'll keep it,"

"I don't believe you."

"I swear."

Blanca was so moved by Otto's words that she made her way to My Corner at a quick pace. Upon entering My Corner, she stopped and looked around. This was her town, the streets where she had spent her childhood and youth. Now everything was wrapped in an alien mist. She felt like a prisoner who had received a short leave and didn't know what to do with it.

In My Corner she was greeted with pleasure, and they rushed to serve her a cup of coffee and a piece of cake. She had planned to ask whether anyone knew of a goldsmith or a jewelry store where she could sell a jewel, but she checked herself.

While Blanca was busy with her thoughts, a short young man approached her. He stood next to her table, his head bent, and for a moment she didn't recognize him. But as soon as she did, she cried out, "Ernst!"

Ernst Schimmer was her great competitor in elementary school and later in high school. He, too, excelled in mathematics and Latin, but he had some sort of inhibition that blocked him and overshadowed his obvious talent. All of his excellent grades always had an annoying "minus" attached to them. The mathematics and Latin teachers liked him and encouraged him, and there were days when he displayed wonders at the blackboard, but then that hidden flaw would appear and spoil the effect. Blanca didn't like Ernst and ignored him. From an early age a bitterness showed itself on his lips, the sign of a person dissatisfied with himself. He suffered in class, especially from Adolf. Adolf used to call him a Jewish slug.

Blanca overcame her muteness. "How are you, Ernst?"

"I came to visit my hometown."

"And where do you live now?"

"In Salzburg."

Fortune had not smiled upon Ernst, either, it seemed. He had studied at the university for a year, but his parents couldn't afford to support him, and he was forced to go out and work. He worked in a children's clothing store in Heimland for a year, but then both of his parents died and he moved to Salzburg. There he was a cashier in a department store. Blanca looked at him and said, "You haven't changed."

"What are you doing?" he asked.

"I live and breathe." The voice of past days returned to her.

"May I join you for a cup of coffee?" Ernst said, sitting down beside her.

No, Ernst hadn't changed. The wrinkles of bitterness had indeed become somewhat deeper, but there was no alteration in his appearance. He spoke as he used to, emphasizing, for some reason, the word "future," a word his parents had apparently used frequently. His parents had been known in the town as hardworking people whom fortune had not favored.

"You haven't converted, have you?" Blanca asked.

"No."

"Like everybody else, I did."

"My parents didn't push me into that, and I myself never felt the need to do it."

"You did right. A person should be loyal to his sentiments," Blanca said, feeling that those words hadn't come out of her own mouth.

"Who knows?" he replied, like someone who has already been burned.

After a pause he added, "When we were children, we competed with each other. People used to say, two competitive Jews. You were better, I must admit."

"Why do you say that?"

"You were more open. Your response to a math problem was spontaneous. You immediately saw the possibilities, and sometimes all the possibilities."

"But you were more thorough."

"Maybe. But I was immersed in unnecessary details."

"Strange, we never talked about it then." For a moment she wanted to stop the stream of words.

"You were brilliant, and I was sure that I couldn't catch up with you. Your quickness, your agility, proved to me every day that I was on a lower level."

It was the same Ernst, with the same inhibitions coming out of hiding. Blanca wanted to contradict him but didn't know how. Once again muteness seized her.

"I have to go back," Ernst said, rising to his feet. She even remembered his way of standing up now. The journey from his seat to the blackboard was an obstacle course for him. On the way his momentum would dwindle, and he would reach the blackboard without any strength, immediately declaring, "I was mistaken. I had an idea, but it turned out to be useless. Excuse me." Because of those apologies, he aroused mockery. In her heart, even Blanca was contemptuous of that weakness of his.

"How long were you here for?" Once again she overcame her muteness.

"Just a few hours. I felt a kind of urge to come, so I did. I took a walk around all the familiar places, but I didn't meet anyone I knew. You're the only one. I didn't want to go inside the high school. That wasn't a place that was pleasant for me."

"And how was your parents' house?"

"Still standing. I sold it very cheaply at the time."

"Ernst, forgive me."

"For what?"

"I didn't know how to appreciate your abilities, and that greatly troubles me. In many areas, you were better than I was."

"You're mistaken."

"I'm not saying it to flatter you."

"I know. But the truth mustn't be ignored."

"In any event, pardon me, if it's not hard for you."

"For what, Blanca?"

"For the bad things I did to you."

"You never did anything bad to me. You were the model I was aspiring to."

"I ignored you."

"Rightly."

"Ernst," she said, not knowing what she intended to say.

"See you soon," he said, and hurried to escape the place.

"Ernst!" she called, stretching out her arms to stop him. But Ernst was already outside, directing his steps toward the train. Blanca didn't move. She didn't remember what she had said or what Ernst had told her. It seemed to her that the injustice that had been done to him years ago was now demanding recompense. True, Adolf had been much harder on Ernst than she had been: once he had beaten Ernst till he bled. When the vice-principal had asked Adolf why he had done it, Adolf replied, "He annoys me. His very existence is annoying." The vice-principal had indeed scolded him, but not very severely.

"Ernst," she said distractedly, trying to stand up.

The café was now full of retired people and idlers. Blanca knew most of them. One of the storekeepers whom she knew well, though she didn't remember his name, turned to her and said, "Your grandmother Carole was a brave woman in a generation when the Jews were fleeing from their Judaism like mice. You can be proud of her."

"I am proud of her."

"She was the only Jewish woman in the city who wasn't ashamed of her Jewishness, and she denounced the converts to Christianity and those who hid their Judaism."

"I know," said Blanca.

"That's not enough," said the storekeeper, rising to his feet. "You have to identify with her publicly."

"But I converted, sir," Blanca whispered.

"Sorry, I didn't know. I'll do it. I'll stand up. Tomorrow. A closed sanctuary is a sign that there is no judgment and no judge."

In the café they knew: the man wouldn't keep his word. He had already made that declaration several times, but this time it had a special sharpness.

Blanca rose and said, "Pardon me."

"I have to beg your pardon," the storekeeper said. "You're exempt from that obligation, but I'm not. I owe it to my father and mother. They were simple, proud Jews."

After Blanca left the café she wandered through the streets, astonished by the wonders that the morning had brought her. At noon she went back home to see how Otto was doing. Otto was pleased and said, "Mama, you're beautiful."

"You're more beautiful."

"I'm still little."

"But you'll be the biggest."

To Kirtzl she said, "I looked for work and didn't find a thing. I'll go to Himmelburg; maybe I'll find something there."

"You must find something," said Kirtzl.

"True," said Blanca, and the thought flashed through her mind:

I'll get rid of her, too, one day. This time Otto didn't wrap himself around her legs. He waved and called out, "Come back soon, Mama."

Blanca reached the station at one o'clock. The train to Himmelburg was late, and she sat at the narrow buffet and saw Ernst again. Now she realized that the inhibition dwelt in his neck. Whenever he was called to the blackboard, his head would bend to the right, the words he was saying would be choked off immediately, and he would start to stammer. His stammer, more than the rest of his movements, attracted mockery. He tried to overcome this defect, but it was, apparently, stronger than his will. Now Blanca remembered those moments with blinding clarity.

50

TIIE TRAIN ARRIVED an hour and a half late. Blanca went to
the buffet car and ordered a drink. At the counter she met the
veteran conductor Brauschwinn, a sturdy man whose bearing had
been crushed by the years, but not his spirit. Every year he had
accompanied Blanca's family on their vacation. He had witnessed
her mother's illness, and during the shivah he had come to console
her father. Then he had watched her father's decline, and he had
tried to ease his mind with old folk sayings. Blanca had told him
about her father's disappearance.

Blanca's parents had liked Brauschwinn. They used to buy their
tickets from him and tip him. Brauschwinn would sit and tell them
about his troubles with his wife, his sons, and his daughters. He
got no joy from any of them—from his wife because she was a
nag, from his daughters because they had left the house and
moved to the big city, and from his sons because they had no ambition, worked like mules, and barely made a living. In his youth
he had spent time with Jews in Vienna. He had worked in their
stores and in their small textile factories. Had it not been for his
wife, who had pulled him to Heimland, he would not have left
Vienna. The provinces were a cage that stained a person's soul, he
said repeatedly.

Brauschwinn loved Jews and didn't hide his love from anyone.
It was a long-standing, devoted, and arbitrary love. The other conductors knew about it and made fun of him, but Brauschwinn
wasn't like other people: if anyone reviled Jews in his presence, he
upbraided them, and if the reviler was particularly impertinent,

he'd get a slap. Because of his love of the Jews, he was called insulting names, but Brauschwinn didn't relent. More than once he had stood on the platform and shouted: You'll be asking their forgiveness soon enough.

Brauschwinn spoke Yiddish without an accent and knew some prayers. He had absorbed the ways of the traditional Jews who had migrated from Galicia to Vienna, and nothing was lost on him. Blanca's father used to tease him with questions, but it didn't faze him. He used to say that there's unusual beauty even in removing all the unleavened foods before Passover. When he learned that Blanca had converted to Christianity and married Adolf, he expressed his disappointment in a single phrase.

"Too bad," he said.

Brauschwinn was pleased to see Blanca now, and in his joy he called out, "Here's Blanca. You haven't changed a bit. Thin as ever."

"And how have you been?"

"Tsoris." He used the Yiddish word he'd learned from the Galician Jews. Grandma Carole had used that word, but Blanca didn't remember exactly what it meant.

"What's the matter?"

"I've been sick."

Blanca didn't ask any more. His face told the whole story, but in his eyes the fire still burned of a man who cherishes precious memories, those of his youth among the Jews of Galicia who had been uprooted from their home ground and exiled to the big city.

"What came afterward wasn't life but leftovers," Brauschwinn had let slip once.

"What attracted you to those Jews?" Blanca dared to ask him this time.

"Their prayer. Have you ever seen Jews praying?"

"I was in the synagogue with my mother a few times."

"Those weren't Jews anymore, my dear. Among the Jews of the east there's a style of prayer, of blessing, and also of human connection."

"Don't the Austrians have any style?"

"They do, but it's clumsy."

Strange, Blanca said to herself. *After all, I was once Jewish.*

Brauschwinn sat and spoke, and the more he told her, the more spiritual his face appeared. It was clear that this simple man who had never set foot in a high school, who had worked hard on trains all those years, whose wife vexed him, who got no joy from his sons and daughters, that this man had a secret that nourished him even at this difficult time, a day before he was to be hospitalized.

"Mr. Brauschwinn," Blanca said, rising to her feet. "Your love for the Jews is a mystery to me."

"They're worthy of it, believe me," he said, removing his cap.

"Will we see each other soon?" she asked when the train stopped at Himmelburg.

"Everything is in the hands of heaven, as people used to say."

In Himmelburg a pleasant summer light filled the streets. The courtyards and roads were bathed in silence. Blanca wished she could go into one of the little cafés, order a cup of coffee and a piece of cheesecake, and sink into her thoughts, the way she used to do. But her legs refused to do her bidding. They drew her to the old age home.

Theresa saw her from a distance.

"Blanca!" she called out.

Blanca noticed immediately that the corridor had been emptied of its residents, and in the dormitory the old people moved like shadows. Theresa told her that the situation in the old age home couldn't be worse. The assistance from Vienna had stopped, and though the Himmelburg community continued to support the home, it didn't have the means to maintain the place. Anyone who had a bit of money ran away. The salaries had been reduced, and they were months in arrears.

They sat in the kitchen, and Theresa served her lunch. She told

Blanca that her husband was ill again and had been hospitalized.
She spent whatever she made on doctors and medicines. There was
never any word from their absent children. Except for her sister,
whom she saw occasionally, she had no close relatives. But one
mustn't complain, she said; anyone who was walking on their own
two feet and not confined to a wheelchair should bless their good
fortune.

Blanca raised her voice. "I felt that I had to come back here."

"When did you have that feeling?"

"Yesterday I saw my father passing before me."

"The dead go to their own world, dear, and we'll see them only
at the great resurrection."

"Sometimes I feel that my father is angry at me."

"You are mistaken. In the world of truth, our parents speak only
on our behalf. They know what we're going through."

It was hard to know whether that was an expression of faith or
a habit of speech that Theresa had inherited from her mother. She
spoke to Blanca the way one speaks to an injured person, to soothe
the pain. Blanca took in the words that Theresa showered on her
but wanted to say, *My guilt feelings can't be healed by folk wisdom.
I'll wallow in them all my life.*

Theresa didn't say any more. Blanca remembered when she first
arrived here with Adolf—how he had surveyed the old people with
wordless contempt, and how he had threatened the director so that
she, in her fear, had agreed to take in Blanca's poor father.

"I have to rescue Otto," Blanca said, rousing herself.

"You have to be patient, to wait and see."

"To wait, you say?"

"They're punished in the end, whether by people or by heaven."

"How many years did you wait?"

"The years pass quickly, and in the end freedom will come. You
mustn't rush things." In her voice Blanca heard a cruel simplicity,
a kind of women's spell that was passed down from generation to

generation, that said again and again, *Wait, wait, until the bastard croaks, and then you, too, can go free and enjoy a new life.*

Before leaving, Blanca asked, "Do you know a goldsmith or a jeweler?"

"Yes," Theresa said, and smiled as though she were sharing another secret. "There's a Jew in this city who has a jewelry store, an honest man. He'll appraise the jewel and pay you its price. He won't cheat you."

"I don't know how to thank you."

"What did I do for you?"

"Once again, you pulled me up out of the underworld."

51

BLANCA LEFT THE old age home and walked directly to the jeweler's shop. She was sure he would stare at her and say, *This is a stolen ring and you're a thief.* But she didn't stop. She walked on, as though in the grip of a force stronger than her fears. To her surprise, the jeweler didn't suspect her. He looked at her with sympathy and asked, "Where are you from, young lady?"

"From Heimland."

"A nice town. What's your name, if I may ask?"

"Blanca Guttmann."

"You're Erwin Guttmann's daughter. What an educated and pleasant man."

"He's no longer with us, I regret to say."

"He used to come here: a man of refinement in the full sense of the word." The jeweler examined the ring from every angle and declared, "It's old and worth four thousand." He paid her with new banknotes, and Blanca made a reckoning: that was a year's salary for work in the old age home. But her joy was marred. The thought that she had used her father's good name to deceive the jeweler stung her. She began walking to the railway station with rapid steps.

On the train, she sat in the buffet car and drank a few brandies. Her head was spinning, and she knew that she would pay for her deed one day, both for the theft and for the deception. Then the dizziness passed, and she fell asleep in her seat.

She returned home at one thirty and told Kirtzl she'd found work. Then she talked with Otto and played with him on the floor.

Otto was happy, as though he understood that from now on his mother would no longer abandon him for long periods of time. An hour later she left the house and hurried to the railway station. First she thought of traveling to Winterweiss, where her parents used to go on vacation, but at the last moment she changed her mind and got off at Hochstein, a small and little-known town. She rented a room in a pension and took a bath. Then she saw Adolf's long arm before her eyes as he raised his belt against her. She felt the dizziness and the heavy stumble that quickly followed, then the effort to rise, then the blurred sensations and the weak knees. For a moment it seemed to her that Adolf was in the corridor, lying in wait for her. She buried her face in her hands, as she did when he whipped her back.

But this time he wasn't there, he wasn't lying in wait. The small, quiet room, filled with houseplants and covered with carpets, seemed to say, *Here no one meddles in anyone else's life. The owner of the pension is a delicate woman who guards the privacy of her tenants.* The thick silence enveloped her, and she fell asleep.

Blanca slept for the rest of the day. When she awakened, she was very thirsty. She hurried to a café and ordered a cup of coffee and some cheesecake. The cake was tasty, and she ordered another slice. She sat in the café for about two hours, and the more she sat, the more her mind was emptied of thoughts. It seemed to her that all the people sitting around her and drinking coffee were much taller than she, and they knew what to do with their lives.

Then she went outside and sat on a bench. The small, unfamiliar town, about two hundred kilometers from her hometown and lit with a summer sun, felt very pleasant to her. For a moment it seemed to her that if she stayed there for a few days, her life would go back to the way it used to be, and everything would start afresh. She saw clearly the two thick mathematics books that her father used to peruse eagerly in his free time. *Everything begins here,* he would say with envy. *Once I, too, had ideas,* she thought, *but they've vanished.* At special times Blanca's father would write out a formula for her and explain the greatness that dwelt within it.

Blanca had planned to go back and see Otto toward the evening. But she didn't. The night was tranquil, and people strolled along the boulevard. The light danced in and out of the trees and brought hidden colors to mind. There was a time when colors like those would wash over her in the evenings and move her to tears. *Mama,* she was about to get up and say, *I haven't gone far away. I'll wait for you.*

Ever since she had left Blumenthal, Blanca had seen her parents with every step she took. Usually they were separate, but sometimes she saw them together, as though they knew that her life was approaching the abyss.

The next day, Blanca sat on the same bench and drank in the light. The longer she sat there, the more she felt that she was shedding the years, that in a little while she would return to the time when she would come home from school and immediately lose herself in her reading.

In the evening she went back to the pension and sank into the bathtub. "Dear God," she called out loud, "in a little while the iron gates will open, and I'll return to my mother and father at Number Five Cedar Street."

At night she dreamed that the train was delayed and that she had arrived late in Blumenthal. Elsa met her at the door and called out, *Here comes the thief!* She immediately began to search Blanca's clothing. Blanca's body was paralyzed, but she could still feel Elsa's bony fingers in her pockets. Policemen were waiting in the next room and put handcuffs on her. *Don't take Otto away from me!* she shouted. Then she woke up.

The next day Blanca returned on the first train, and Otto was happy.

"I knew you'd come," he said.

"And how are you, my dear?"

"I arranged the soldiers in rows, and now they're guarding the king."

"You arranged them very nicely."

"Mama, play dominoes with me."

"Right away," she said and knelt down.

They played on the floor, and Kirtzl didn't interfere. Later Otto counted to twenty, added and subtracted, and amused himself with his fingers. Blanca pretended to make mistakes, and Otto corrected her.

Later she went back to the train station and took off with no destination in mind. The harvested summer fields sped by and lulled her into a deep sleep. Blanca slept without interruption, not waking until the last stop. Then she hurried away to rent a room in an inn. The small inns, quiet and clean, made her think of an inner life that belonged solely to herself, one that no stranger had a part in. Blanca sat in cafés for hours and drank cup after cup of coffee. Sometimes she also had a drink of brandy, but never very much. For a moment she saw herself in Vienna, already in the third year in the mathematics department. After lunch she would sit in a café and read from the works of Adalbert Stifter. Her mother and father wanted to surprise her and came to visit. They were proud of her achievements. In a little while she would publish an article of her own in the well-known magazine *Papyrus*. Her father kept saying, *I knew. I always knew.*

Thus she sat and daydreamed.

On Saturday Blanca returned home and told Adolf that she had found work in a small old age home near Himmelburg. Adolf, who had drunk a great deal but wasn't intoxicated, immediately asked, "How much are they paying you?" Blanca had prepared a few banknotes. She put them on the table and said, "More than in Blumenthal." Adolf beamed, as though he'd been offered tasty food.

Adolf sat in his seat and Blanca served him dinner. But then, in the middle of the meal, his expression changed. He told her that two Jews had recently bought the dairy and that they wanted to lengthen the workday. The workers had declared a strike, and they were planning to attack the owners. Adolf despised Jews in general, but this time he was able to articulate his animosity.

"We'll eliminate them," he said, his mind finally at rest.

After the meal Adolf went to join his friends at the tavern. Blanca sat with Otto and told him that soon they'd be taking a long trip. Otto asked for details, and Blanca soared off in her imagination. Then they played dominoes, and Otto won twice. For a long time he played by himself, too, had imaginary adventures, and murmured to himself. Finally he fell asleep on the floor.

Late that night Adolf returned drunk and angry and immediately started reviling the Jews, who were destroying the Austrian economy and filling their pockets with money. Blanca made an awkward movement and knocked over a china pot. That drove Adolf out of his senses. He slapped her face and called her a careless woman who broke things without consideration. Blanca, who had learned not to react, responded this time.

"What are you talking about?" she said.

Adolf grabbed her arm and shook her, shouting, "Who said, 'What are you talking about?' Who dared to say, 'What are you talking about?'"

Blanca, in great pain and anger, shouted back, "Murderer! Leave me alone." Then Adolf started kicking her, and his fury didn't subside until he'd knocked her down.

That night Blanca didn't sleep. The blows that Adolf had dealt her hurt and burned, but, to her surprise, she didn't feel weakness. She felt that if she had to leave, she would, and she would even be able to carry a burden on her back. She went to see Otto, who was sleeping soundly. Then she went over to the window. The darkness was dense, and no light was visible anywhere. She thought of going outdoors and sitting on the front steps, but the thought vanished, and she did nothing.

When the first light appeared, the pain attacked her again. She rose from the sofa and dressed her wounds with bandages that Dr. Nussbaum had given her. Her arm was bleeding. She placed a thick cloth on it and tied it with a bandage. She was about to return to the sofa when she saw the ax blade flash. The ax stood in the corner next to the kitchen. Adolf used it to chop wood for heating. Once he had also used it to make fence posts. The ax had a broad blade and a short handle. Blanca walked to the corner and picked it up. It wasn't heavy.

Then Blanca went into the bedroom. Adolf was lying on his back, with his face and chest exposed. His mouth was open, and his breathing was a bit heavy. Blanca raised the ax and with a powerful motion brought the blade down on Adolf's neck. His huge body trembled, and his head fell against the wall. Blood spurted onto her face, and she wiped it with her sleeve.

Blanca ran to Otto's room, changed her clothes, and packed a few things. Then she woke and dressed Otto, and they left for the railway station. The strength Blanca had felt before flowed out of her, and her knees trembled.

"Where are we going, Mama?"

"We're going on a trip."

The morning train came on time, and no one was in the station. They entered a car and sat next to the window. Blanca's thoughts were spinning, but she knew that she should get off at Blitzstein because at eight o'clock the express train left from there. There were not many passengers at Blitzstein, either. The express train hurtled out of the station.

"Mama." Otto opened his eyes.

"What, dear?"

"Where are we going?"

"We're going north."

Otto closed his eyes and curled up on the seat.

The express train stopped at Hochstein. They transferred to a small local train that stopped at village stations and sawmills. Blanca reasoned that no one would know what had happened until the afternoon, and the farther she got, the harder it would be for the police to find her.

"Where are we, and where are we going?" Otto kept asking. Blanca would distract him, confuse him, deceive his limited memory.

"We'll live on the train," she said at one point. "What could be better than that?"

Otto immediately showered her with questions. Blanca answered in a haphazard way, contradicting herself, mixing up day and night. Finally she said, "Why are you tormenting your mother, dear?"

"What's 'tormenting,' Mama?"

"Nothing, dear." She was too tired to explain.

So they traveled for many days. When they finally stopped and rented the house near the Dessel River, Blanca realized that she no longer had the strength to go on. She sank deeper and deeper into writing. Now, when she began to sense danger again, all her fears were reawakened. Blanca wrapped up the manuscript and said, "This is for you, Otto."

"But I only know how to read a little."

"Soon you'll know more."

52

THE FOLLOWING DAY the landlady came, and Blanca paid her rent, adding an extra banknote. The landlady brought a present for Otto: a vest that she herself knitted. Blanca hugged her and promised to write. Their bags were already packed, and the landlady stood in the doorway and followed them with her eyes until they reached the station.

Before long they were on their way. Otto was pleased. The sight of the tall trees and the lakes excited him, and he didn't stop expressing amazement. Blanca was saddened. The fear that had died down during the past weeks pounded at her once more. She wasn't afraid of her own death, but she was afraid for Otto. Since he had asked, "Why won't you tell me what's written in the notebook?" it seemed to her that he knew her secret. Again she tried to distract him, but this time the words failed her. During the weeks they'd spent near the water, he had grown and become tan, and his vocabulary was richer. On their last walk he had asked how birds fly without falling. Blanca, who had once studied the physics of bird flight in school, had forgotten the answer. She was flustered and finally raised her hands, saying, "I can't remember a thing."

How much those days near the river had changed her, Blanca did not yet know. But she had become stronger, and some of her essence had found its way into Otto. She was certain that little of Adolf remained in him and that she would be able to wipe out whatever was still there. She had noticed that he used expressions like "it may be assumed" and "nevertheless." And sometimes, when his mind was not at ease, he would say, "It's hard for me to believe." All of those expressions were hers. Adolf had never used them. She was more and more certain that in the fullness of time, Otto would change completely and would indeed be like her mother's brother, whose name he bore.

"Uncle Otto, whom you're named after, was an excellent student at the university."

"What happened to him?"

"He died." She didn't conceal it now.

"And we'll meet him in the world of sleep?"

"Correct."

Several times Otto had asked about death, and Blanca had avoided answering in detail. Once she said, "Death is a long sleep." Otto accepted her words and didn't bother her about the matter again.

Meanwhile, they pushed on, changing trains, and if they saw a pleasant village, they would stop there, rent a room or a house, bathe, rest, and set out again the next day.

After they had left the flat plains and proceeded up the mountains, Otto slept a lot. When he awoke, Blanca would tell him about the marvels of the east, about her friend Sonia, and about the Carpathians. Otto asked many questions, and Blanca described everything she knew at length and everything her imagination had embroidered.

"And we won't go to church anymore?"

"No."

Once she scolded him for asking about church and said, "The churches are crude, and our feet won't enter them." But about the little wooden synagogues, which she had encountered in Martin Buber's book, she told him a great deal. For some reason Otto pictured the Jews of the Carpathians in his imagination as hard-working dwarfs. Blanca corrected him and said, "They're the same height as everyone else. Maybe a little shorter, but not dwarfs by any means."

"Why did they look like dwarfs to me?"

"That's my fault. I didn't describe them properly."

They traveled farther and farther. What was left of the summer still gilded the landscape here and there. Though the grain had been harvested, apples ripened in orchards, and on the slopes the plum trees bent under the weight of their fruit. Blanca had a great desire to get off at one of the deserted stations and absorb some of the silence, but when she saw how pleased Otto was in his sleep, she gave up the idea.

Suddenly Otto woke up and said, "I'm afraid."

"Of what, dear?"

"I fell into a deep pit."

"It just seems that way to you. It was a dream. The train is moving along very nicely. We've already gone quite a distance, and in a little while we'll reach the station. At the station we'll buy fruit and lemonade."

Blanca suddenly knew that her life in this world would be very short and that she had to take care of Otto. During the weeks that they had spent in the house near the Dessel River, thoughts of death disturbed her. Now she sensed that the danger was once more at hand. And she wasn't mistaken: there, in the small station in the town of Schlossberg, Blanca saw the notice hanging on the wall.

"Wanted throughout the empire," it read, "a woman named Blanca Hammer, who brutally murdered her husband, Adolf Hammer. The woman, of average height, thin, with dark gray eyes, ran away with her son, Otto. Anyone who has seen her or knows of her whereabouts is requested to inform the nearest police station immediately. The emperor's police will be grateful to him for his good citizenship. We are commanded to extirpate evil from among us."

Blanca's face darkened. That which her heart had told her was written on the wall.

"Give Mama your hand," she said to Otto. "We're leaving for the east immediately."

"Is it far from here?"

"No."

"Can we ride a boat on the river?"

"Certainly."

"And are there small horses?"

"I suppose so."

"Why are you in a hurry, Mama?"

"I'm not in a hurry, dear."

Good God, Blanca said to herself. *Otto doesn't know what's in store for his mother. They hang murderers two hours before sunrise, in the dark, without ceremony and without mercy.*

53

ONCE AGAIN THE trains bore them from place to place. At the larger villages, the train would stop, take on masses of peasants, and rush off. From the train windows Blanca saw the WANTED posters on the walls, and she was sure that her life was in greater and greater danger with every passing hour.

"Otto."

"What?"

"You have to be strong."

"I am strong."

Blanca knew that the moment they caught her she would be separated from Otto. They would send him back to his aunts, and they would try her and send her to the gallows. His aunts would drill into him, morning, noon, and night, that his mother was a murderer and that his memory of her must be erased. Otto would refuse to believe them at first, but in time he would be convinced. The police would read the notebooks. They would present them as evidence at the trial, they would eventually be buried in an archive, and no one would remember her anymore. Suddenly she felt sad for herself and for her life, which had gone awry.

"When you grow up, don't forget the notebooks. I'm leaving them in your backpack," Blanca said, knowing there was no logic to her words.

Otto raised his eyes and said, "I'll read them as soon as I'm big."

Blanca kissed his forehead. "I'm very proud of you," she said.

They arrived in Czernowitz. Blanca had planned to look for a kindergarten for Otto, but she immediately realized that their name would betray him. Not only that, Czernowitz was a big city, and gendarmes swarmed over every corner. Better to go farther, to a more modest place.

The posters stood out on the walls. She had never before seen her name in such big printed letters, and she was momentarily filled with a fear that was mingled with a malicious pleasure. *Everybody's looking for me,* she thought, *and I'm here, in the very heart of the city, next to police headquarters.*

Now she remembered that she had heard about Czernowitz for the first time from her mother. As a little girl, Blanca's mother had passed through Czernowitz with her family on her way from Galicia to Austria. The city had been etched in her mother's memory because of the splendid stores and the cafés known for their fine strawberry tortes. Blanca wanted very much to spend at least an hour in the place where her mother had walked, to stroll with Otto along Herrengasse, which was famous for its charm, but her fear was stronger than her desire.

"We won't visit this busy city," she said to Otto, and they quickly boarded a train for the provinces.

"What's your name, dear?" They were alone in the car, and Blanca surprised Otto with this question as soon as the train departed.

"Otto Hammer. Why are you asking?"

"That's a mistake. That was your name when you were little. Now that you're big, you'll have a grown-up name."

"When will I get the new name?"

"Right away. I'll tell you your new name right away: Otto Guttmann. Do you hear?"

"Will that be my new name?" Otto asked, smiling.

"Yes. You have reached the age of four and a quarter. When a child reaches the age of four and a quarter, his mother gives him a new name, and he immediately forgets his old name. What's your name, dear?"

"My name is Otto Guttmann."

"Correct. You have to practice saying it to yourself from now on: My name is Otto Guttmann. Everything that used to be is as if it never was."

The end of the summer was brightly colored, and more than once Blanca said to herself, *We'll get off here, we'll burrow into the thick shrubs and live in nature.* But every time she grabbed Otto's hand to get off, she was deterred. At one station she yielded to temptation, and they did get out. Except for a small kiosk and a few drunkards gathered around it, there was nothing. They drank lemonade, bought a basket of plums, and without delay boarded the next train.

Otto slept, and Blanca was glad of it. It seemed to her that as long as he was asleep, she was protected. The trains in this region were slow and neglected. More than once the train stopped and stood in place for an hour or two. The conductors got off and sat by the kiosk, drinking lemonade and smoking with pleasure, as though time meant nothing. But in fact, that relaxation frightened Blanca. It was as though the tiger were about to leap out of the thicket. While the train was speeding along, Otto's sleep was pure and quiet. But when the train stopped and the conductors got off, Otto's face filled with curiosity, and he started to pester her with questions. So that he would stop asking, Blanca told him stories. At first she had wanted to tell him a little about what she had written in the notebook, but she understood right away that Otto might get confused and mix up Adolf's family with hers. It would be better for his life to begin, for the moment, alongside the Dessel River and on the trains, and no earlier.

"Otto," she said.

"What, Mama?"

"Don't worry. The train will start moving soon."

"I'm not worried."

"Then why does your face look worried?"

"I remembered the banks of the Dessel."

"That's a marvelous place, and we have to remember it forever. What do you see now?"

"The red fish."

"True, the water was very clear, and we could see the fish, but the plants were also beautiful. Everything was beautiful. So why are you worried?"

"Will we go back there?"

"One day, I suppose."

"I'd like to go back there."

In her heart she was glad that the new sights were gradually adhering to his soul and that she wouldn't have to fool him or lie.

"Otto," she said.

"What, Mama?"

"Will you forgive me?"

"For what?"

"For all the crimes that I committed."

"What are crimes?"

"Don't you know?"

"No."

54

"STRUZHINCZ!" THE CONDUCTOR announced. The sound penetrated Blanca's sleep, and it woke her. She immediately gripped Otto's hand and said, "We're getting off."

"Where?" asked Otto, still tangled in sleep.

"This is it," she said, without knowing what she was saying.

Here, too, Blanca saw two big posters glued to a wall, each proclaiming the name and description of the murderer. This time the letters were in red, making them stand out even more. Blanca looked at them, lowered her eyes, and slipped out of the station.

Cold evening light illuminated the street and the low houses. Her eyes immediately picked out a sign: SALZBURG HOTEL. Nearby there was another sign: VIENNA HOTEL. The buildings looked as though they housed well-run hotels. But in a hotel they write down your address and ask questions. Then, in an alley not far away, Blanca saw a modest sign: FAMILY PENSION, PERSONAL SERVICE, REASONABLE PRICES. The alley pleased her. The people walked slowly, the calm of the evening permeating their gait. A familiar but forgotten tranquillity flowed from the open windows.

"It's good that we came here," she said.

"Mama," Otto called out, confused from the long journey.

"What, dear?"

"I'd like to eat something good."

"In a little while they'll serve us dinner," she said, picturing in her mind a set table. It turned out to be a Jewish-owned pension. Blanca remembered the little Jewish sanitariums in the mountains where her mother had been hospitalized. The owners had been gentle people, somewhat similar to their patients.

"My name is Blanca Guttmann, and this is my son, Otto Guttmann," Blanca said, introducing herself.

"Did you come from Czernowitz?"

"Yes, we did."

"How long will you be here, if I may ask?"

"A month, maybe longer." Blanca spoke in relaxed tones to avoid
raising questions.

"My name is Tina Tauber," said the landlady. "My German
isn't perfect, but my husband studied it in high school, and he
speaks without mistakes. He corrects my errors, but without much
success. What can I do? I was born in a village where we spoke
Yiddish."

The woman was about forty, and it was evident that contact
with strangers embarrassed her. Her husband, who came to help,
did indeed speak a fine German. He showed them their room and
said, "Come downstairs with me, and we'll serve you dinner. You're
surely hungry. What's your name, little boy?"

Blanca intervened and said, "Otto is big already. Otto is four. In
a little while he'll attend kindergarten."

After many days of displacement, fear, and depression, the dining room seemed like a quiet return to a familiar place. The meal
included vegetables, cheese and sour cream, and thick coffee. The
fragrance of the coffee reminded Blanca of the shaded country
cafés where she had sat with her parents. For a moment she forgot
the jolting journey, and she clung to those vanished places as if she
had never left them.

"You've come on vacation?" Mrs. Tauber asked cautiously.

"Yes, indeed. We need it, like one needs air to breathe."

"During this time of year it's very quiet here," Mrs. Tauber said
calmly.

"Thank you," said Blanca.

"I haven't done anything for you yet." The woman spoke the
way they did in the country.

That night Blanca slept without bad dreams. In her sleep she saw Otto, tall and thin like her uncle Otto, whom her mother had loved and loved to talk about. When Blanca awoke, it was already late. Otto was still sleeping, curled up next to her. *They're looking for me in railroad stations,* she thought, *but I'm here with Otto and no one will discover me because this place is out of the way and hidden.* Now the room revealed itself to her: tall, narrow windows, two old-fashioned dressers, an armchair, and two wicker chairs. In the corner was a desk.

"We're lazy. It's nine o'clock," she said as soon as Otto woke up.

"Where are we going?" he asked as if he were on a train.

"We're not leaving. We're here."

"Is there a river?"

"I suppose so, but it's autumn now, and the water is cold."

"What will we do?"

"We'll read and play and do a lot of other things."

Mrs. Tauber greeted them with a "Good morning" and said, "Make yourselves at home. Here's what I can offer you for breakfast. Everything is hot and fresh."

They ate and drank. Otto was impressed by the polished copper pots on the stove, from which you could easily remove omelets and cheese dumplings dipped in strawberry jam. Blanca sipped the thick coffee, which seeped into her like a restorative potion.

She remembered what she had practiced with Otto, and drilled it into him again. "Otto is four and a quarter. Otto is big now. His name is Otto Guttmann, and in a little while he'll go to kindergarten."

Otto raised his eyes and stared at her as though he had caught his mother doing something foolish.

After breakfast Otto said, "Mama, let's go out for a walk." Blanca was somewhat apprehensive about the new place, but she overcame her misgivings and said, "We'll go out right away and see what there is here."

First they strolled down the main avenue and then they sat in a little café and ordered ice cream. There was a toy store near the café, and Blanca bought Otto a basket full of toys. Otto was pleased and expressed his joy by clapping his hands.

Then they sat in a public park, and Otto played. The park was clean, and Blanca knelt down and played with him.

"I have a lot of toys!" he cried out, confused because so many toys had suddenly come to him.

After a while Blanca said, "Today we'll buy new clothes, too. It's already autumn, and you have no warm clothing."

"And boots, too?"

"Boots, too, like grown-ups wear."

And so they did. By the afternoon, Otto was equipped for the winter. When they returned, Mrs. Tauber was pleased to see them and said, "You've come just in time. Lunch is ready."

For lunch she served them borscht with sour cream and stuffed eggplant.

"We have no fish today," she apologized.

"That's all right," said Blanca. "Otto will be going to kindergarten soon. I'm sure they have fish there."

The landlady stared at her and said nothing.

After lunch, Otto busied himself with his new toys, and Blanca lay down on the bed and observed him. She felt that a part of her had been left behind in the enchanted cabin on the banks of the Dessel and that from now on she would have to live without some vital organs. *My life has to contract,* she said to herself, *and the more it contracts, the better it will be.* An old sadness, one that had gnawed at her years ago in high school, arose within her. *In a short while these eyes of mine will see no more. This room and its modest furniture won't remember that I was here and watched Otto play. And Otto, too, will be so immersed in his own life that he won't remember these magical moments.*

"Otto," she blurted out.

"What, Mama?"

"You have to be strong."

"I'm strong."

"That's exactly what I wanted to hear," she said, and was sorry she had said it.

Indeed, Otto sank deeper and deeper into his new toys. The evening light streamed through the tall windows and shone dimly on the floor. Blanca felt that she had distanced herself very far from her life, that she was exposed and without wings to shelter her. In her second-to-last year of high school they had read *The Brothers Karamazov* and discussed it. They had spoken about the soul and about its darkness, about good and evil, and about murder, which was forbidden in any event. About God, for some reason, they had not spoken. One of the girls, not one of the outstanding students, had surprised everyone by speaking explicitly about God, and the literature teacher, a pleasant, enlightened man, had made a dismissive gesture with his right hand, as if to say, *Why drag our feet into intangible things? They won't be of any use to us. Let's talk about visible and palpable things. There, at least, we're on firm footing.* The girl, whose name Blanca didn't remember now, bowed her head, and her face flushed as if she had been slapped. The unfortunate girl's face now appeared clearly before her, as though the insult had just been hurled at her.

Blanca knelt down and played dominoes with Otto. Otto won, but he wasn't happy with his victory. It seemed to him that his mother was fooling him, though Blanca assured him again and again that his victory was truly earned, that she had done nothing to let him win.

Then Otto put on his new clothes. They suited him. He looked like the only son of a petit bourgeois family that had lost its fortune, but whose mother decided to dress him like a prince anyway, and to that end she had taken out a loan, unbeknownst to her husband. Now, sudden fear fell upon her.

———

Later in the day Blanca remembered the hasty visit she had made to the cemetery during the winter, after Otto's recovery. No one had been there, and heavy rain whipped the gravestones. The mud on the paths was deep and sticky, and Blanca could barely reach her mother's grave. When she stood before the small tombstone, she had nothing to say, and she immediately turned back in her tracks. Since that visit, she hadn't dared return. It seemed to her that her mother was asking her not to come and bother her, as she had done a few weeks before her death.

"My darlings, let me be by myself for a few days," she had said at the time. "I have to be by myself." Blanca's father, who was confused and fearful, had grasped Blanca's hand, stepped back to the door, and murmured, "We're going right out. We won't disturb you. You need rest." Years had passed since she had heard those trembling words. Now they filled her ears again.

Otto played and played until he finally sank down and slept. From the time he had been a baby, Blanca loved to watch Otto in his sleep. Now he slept in a different position. He lay folded up, and it was evident that his daytime activity was continuing on into his sleep. His intense face softened, and a thin smile spread across it. Blanca sat without moving from her place. The thought that she, with her own hands, had freed Otto from the prison of Kirtzl, had borne him far away and brought him here—that thought filled her with pride.

Suddenly Otto woke up in alarm.

"Mama!" he called out.

"What's the matter, dear?"

"I dreamed that I lost you in a railway station."

"That's not true. I'm here."

"Why didn't I see you?"

"That happens sometimes. It was only a dream."

To distract him, they went down to the dining room and sat in their usual places. It was eight o'clock, and Mrs. Tauber said, "I see that our young man fell asleep and slept well. Now I'll make him something that he'll like a lot: cheese dumplings dipped in strawberry jam. I speak poor German, but you understand me, don't you?"

During that time of the year the guests were few and the dining room was mostly empty, so Mrs. Tauber indulged those who were there. Otto was pleased and ate with gusto. The pension reminded Blanca of another house in another place, but where, she couldn't remember. She sat and drank cup after cup of coffee. The thoughts that had oppressed her during the day had scattered now, and she watched Otto closely. A feeling that things would be like this from now on, that nothing would separate them, throbbed within her.

"What are you thinking about, Mama?" Otto asked softly.

"Nothing."

"You're not thinking about anything?" He tried to understand.

"That happens sometimes."

Otto chuckled, as though he had caught his mother once again in a kind of mental lapse.

55

THE NEXT DAY Blanca learned from Mrs. Tauber that a Jewish woman had recently opened a kindergarten on the outskirts of the city. She had studied in Vienna and was applying modern educational methods. *I must find a secure shelter for Otto,* she said to herself, and so they went there.

It was an old-fashioned house. The windows were broad, there was a garden behind the house, and beyond the fence were open fields. Blanca introduced herself.

"My name is Blanca Guttmann," she said, "and this is my son, Otto Guttmann. We heard about your kindergarten, and we'd like to learn more."

"My name is Rosa Baum," the woman answered. "This is actually the community orphanage."

"That's exactly what I'm looking for," Blanca said. "I can help out here, if there's a need."

"Regrettably, we can't offer a salary."

"I don't need a salary."

So Blanca and Otto were received in "The Home," which is what Rosa called it.

"The place is just right for Otto," Blanca told Mrs. Tauber that evening. "The house is close to the fields, and light streams in from the windows. I'm so grateful to you."

"I didn't do anything," Mrs. Tauber said, blushing.

"You helped us," Blanca insisted. "Without your help, we were like blind people."

Mr. Tauber, in contrast to his wife, spoke in torrents, interpreting and explaining, and his efforts to please the guests were somewhat ridiculous. Despite this, he also had a certain charm, especially when he appeared in the morning with the coffeepot in his hand, loudly announcing his wish to be of service.

"Fresh coffee," he would say. "I prepared it with my own hands just now."

Rosa Baum was about thirty-five years old, but her face was like a young girl's. When she knelt, she was no taller than the children who surrounded her. She herself had been orphaned at a young age, and good people had adopted her and taken care of her schooling. When she was eighteen, they had sent her to Vienna to study education at a well-known institution named after Rousseau. She studied there for five years. At the end of her studies she was invited to stay on and teach, but Rosa wanted to come back to Struzhincz and establish the first orphanage in the province. At the beginning it wasn't easy. For many months she knocked on the doors of wealthy people until she found a donor, Dr. Haussmann, and he placed a beautiful home at her disposal. The daily needs and the salaries were paid for by the Jewish community.

In the mornings Blanca helped to wash the children and to prepare the prayer hall. The prayers lasted no longer than twenty minutes, and afterward breakfast was served.

"I never learned the Hebrew alphabet," Blanca apologized.

"It's not hard to learn, if you want to," said Rosa in the manner of a person who has known sorrow in her life.

"And my knowledge of Judaism, I'm ashamed to say, is extremely limited," said Blanca. She remembered the thick holiday prayer book she had seen in her mother's hands, and its yellowed pages.

Otto felt comfortable in the orphanage. He played with the

children on the floor. They spoke a mixture of Yiddish and German, and he usually understood what they were talking about. Sometimes, when he didn't understand a word, he raised his head, looked over to his mother, and Rosa explained it to him.

At ten thirty Rosa would tell them a Bible story. When Rosa was speaking, the children were very attentive, devouring every word. Afterward they would return to their play in the central room or on the balcony. When a quarrel broke out—and a quarrel did break out once or twice a day—Rosa would stand in the middle of the room, close her eyes, and say, "God in heaven sees everything and hears everything. He is our father and our redeemer, and He commands us to love one another." Amazingly, the quarrel would die down.

At first Blanca was put off by Rosa's religiosity—it seemed contrived to her—but now she saw that her worship of God was neither artificial nor bitter. There was simplicity in her ways and in her faith, and that faith is what she sought to instill in the children.

During one break Rosa said to Blanca, "I'm trying to bring the children close to the faith of their fathers. A person who is connected with the faith of his fathers is not an orphan."

"Will they be religious children?" Blanca asked, immediately sensing that there was a flaw in her question.

"We teach them how to pray," Rosa replied.

"In my house we didn't observe the tradition," said Blanca, realizing that it wasn't the full truth.

In the afternoon Blanca would go down to the market and buy groceries for The Home. The market extended out over a broad, bustling plaza. Peasants displayed their produce in improvised stalls or on long linen cloths. The bustle filled Blanca with a marvelous feeling of forgetfulness, and for a moment it seemed to her that she hadn't just arrived in Struzhincz, but that she had been working in The Home and shopping in this market for years. Toward evening she would return from the market, laden, and lay the baskets on the mats next to the sink. She would prepare supper together with Rosa.

At night Blanca would return to the pension, and Otto would stay and sleep with the children in The Home. Mrs. Tauber was childless, and the sorrow this caused her was apparent in everything she did. Years ago she had traveled to a well-known doctor in Vienna. He had treated her and promised wonders, but later it became known that his methods were fraudulent and that he had deceived hundreds of women. Since then she had not gone anywhere else to seek a cure. For twenty years she and her husband had run the pension. They had regular clients who came from Czernowitz.

"Our needs are not many," she would say, "and our life is simple. For what we have, we say a blessing."

It was evident that the faith of her fathers, which she had brought from her village, sustained her here, too, and there was an innocence in her speech. Nevertheless, Blanca refrained from revealing even a hint of her secret to her. She merely said, "I married very young, and my life wasn't easy. Now I have to bring Otto to a safe haven."

Thus November passed. In early December Blanca noticed that the WANTED posters that had hung on the walls of the railway station were now displayed on public buildings as well. For a few days she tried to ignore them, but they cried out from every wall.

I have to tell you something important, she was about to say to Rosa, but she checked herself. She was afraid and didn't know what to do. It seemed to her that gendarmes were lying in wait for her in every corner.

December was gloomy and cold. After work she would return to the pension and ask, "Has anything come for me?"

"No, nothing, my dear," Mrs. Tauber would reply.

She would go up to her room immediately, curl up in bed, and say to herself, *Otto is so busy with his friends that if I disappear, he won't notice my absence.*

Blanca's life seemed to have slowly disintegrated. First her conversion, then the hasty marriage, and, immediately afterward, her mother's death. In those two ceremonies and in the funeral, parts of her soul were amputated. And after her father's disappearance, her body was emptied of all its will. Just one desire remained within her now: for drink. She tried not to drink in Otto's presence. She would drink only at night, when she was by herself.

"Don't forget the notebooks that are in your backpack," she would remind Otto whenever she was with him.

"What notebooks?"

"The notebooks that I wrote for you."

"I won't forget," said Otto distractedly.

Blanca knew that her requests were pointless. Still, she confused and embarrassed him with them.

With every passing day, the threat to Blanca increased. One evening, when she was on her way from the market to the orphanage, she noticed that a WANTED poster also appeared on the church wall. The sight of the poster on the wall brought before her a vision of Adolf, kneeling in church. Even while kneeling he stood out; he was so much taller than the other worshippers. He didn't pray much, but he did pray loudly. His mother, who always knelt at his side, would sometimes raise her head to gaze at him during the service. She adored him, and showed it even in church.

The next morning, by chance, Blanca heard a woman say to her friend, "Did you hear about the murderess who killed her husband with an ax? They say that she's hiding among us and that a contingent of gendarmes is due to come here to make a search."

"I didn't hear that."

"But you did hear about the murderess?"

"Of course."

"It's frightening to think that she's among us."

They kept on talking, but Blanca couldn't catch their words. She fled and headed straight for the pension.

That night Blanca didn't sleep. The fear that had secretly tormented her suddenly vanished. Her senses were alert, and she could see clearly—the residents of the old age home in Blumenthal, for example. She saw the row of beds in the dormitory, the private rooms of the wealthier residents, and the alcove where the aged Tsirl lived. She had started stealing there by chance, but she soon came to steal deftly, while pretending to be a lethargic woman. The residents hadn't suspected her but picked on the cleaning women instead. All the time she worked there, she had remained on guard and hadn't erred even with a single gesture. And when she bade good-bye to the residents, her voice hadn't conveyed even a single hint of remorse. On the contrary, the pocket full of jewels filled her with hidden pleasure. *This, too, is Blanca,* she said to herself, *and she'll face judgment for that as well, when the day comes.*

The next morning she told Mrs. Tauber, "I've just gotten news that my father is very ill, and I have to set out right away."

"What can I say?" Mrs. Tauber said in a choked voice.

"I didn't behave well toward my father. You should never send parents to an old age home. Old age homes stifle and humiliate people."

Mrs. Tauber cut her short. "Go easy on yourself, Blanca."

"I'm not the essence of purity," Blanca replied.

"None of us has done his duty properly," said Mrs. Tauber.

"I'm not talking about duties, but about ugly selfishness."

Mrs. Tauber was stunned by Blanca's words and refused to accept payment for the final week. But Blanca insisted and said, "I don't want to be in your debt." She also stuffed a banknote into the housekeeper's apron. And so they parted.

When Blanca reached The Home, she went over to the children's beds to see Otto, and for the moment she forgot her hasty departure from the pension. Then she busied herself with work, washing the children and polishing their shoes, preparing the main room for prayers. Rosa had introduced a lovely custom: she decorated the prayer room with flowers and potted plants, and before the prayers began she watered them.

After prayers, Blanca prepared breakfast with Rosa. Only when the meal was finished did she say, "My father is very ill, and I have to leave."

"What's the matter with him?"

"When I parted from my father, he was healthy and in good spirits. He's a professional mathematician. But now I don't know."

"Where is he?"

"In Kimpolung." Blanca wasn't flustered by the question and was pleased that the name had immediately occurred to her.

"Go, Blanca. Otto can stay here. The children like him."

"I don't know how to thank you."

"You don't have to thank me. Let's pray together that God will send a full recovery to your father and to all the sick people among the Jews."

"What should I say to Otto?"

"Tell him the truth. It's always best to tell the truth."

After lunch Blanca knelt and said, "Otto."

"What?" he asked, without looking up.

"I want to tell you something."

"What?"

"I have to go away again."

"Okay."

"I'll return soon. Don't worry."

She expected Otto to pick up his head and look at her, but Otto was too deeply immersed in his play. The words passed by without touching him. Later, too, when she was dressed for the trip, her bundle in her hand, even then he didn't pay attention to her.

Blanca closed the door. Through the panes of glass she could still see Otto's face in profile and a drop on the tip of his nose. She had a huge desire to go back and touch his face again and wipe his nose, but the hand that had closed the door no longer had the power to open it again.

56

FROM THEN ON Blanca traveled without much of a plan. If she chanced upon a wagon, she would pay the driver and hitch a ride. At first the broad fields made her despair, and more than once she was about to return to Struzhincz. *I'd be better off dying near Otto and not in a strange land,* she said to herself, knowing there was no logic to her words. After a while she overcame that delusion and would repeat to herself, *You mustn't go back. Otto has to get used to living without you.*

Along the way she met decent people who helped her and put her up in their homes, and bullies who mistreated her. Against the bullies Blanca struggled with all her might, scratching and cursing. One night she fought off a drunken peasant, biting his arm and hissing at him, "If you touch me, I'll murder you." The peasant panicked and let her go.

I have to keep going, she said to herself, and did so. The winter winds dulled her fear and bolstered her courage. She felt strength in her legs. Sometimes she would stop next to a stream, wash her face, and immediately sink down into the grass and fall asleep. Sometimes a sheep or colt would emerge from the undergrowth. In that green wasteland they looked like hunted creatures to her, running away from the arms of the oppressor, as she was. For a moment they would look at each other and try to draw near, but in the end each would go his own way, as though agreeing that they would be better off alone.

Sometimes she would happen upon a Jewish peddler. He would tell her about the surrounding villages, and she would ask him how to reach a Jewish inn. These thin and unpleasant Jews were her friends now, and she trusted them and bought matches and supplies from them. The life she had left behind now seemed to her like the abandoned ruins she encountered on her way: barren and full of damp darkness.

Then a heavy snow began to fall, and Blanca was fortunate enough to find a warm and hospitable Jewish inn.

"My parents were born not far from here, and in their youth they moved to Austria," she told the owner. "They didn't observe the tradition, but I read the stories of the Hasidim that were collected by Martin Buber, and I would like to see Hasidim close up."

The innkeeper smiled. She had never heard of Martin Buber, but as for Hasidim, "All of us here are Hasidim," she said.

"And where does the Tsadik live?"

"Not far away, in Vizhnitz."

"I didn't know I was so close to him."

The innkeeper didn't know how to behave with her strange guest. She had seen assimilated Jews in her lifetime, but she had never met an assimilated Jew who traveled to see the Tsadik.

Although Vizhnitz was not far off, the way there was hard and strewn with impediments. Gendarmes lay in wait at every crossroad, and thugs gathered in the entrances of taverns. But Blanca was no longer afraid. A powerful resentment seethed within her and filled her arms with strength. For some reason it seemed to her that if she reached Vizhnitz, the snarl of her life would become untangled and she would be set free.

But Blanca's strength did not always sustain her. She was raped once, and once she was beaten by an old peasant who suspected that she had stolen eggs from his chicken coop. Her body bruised, her arms scratched, she would sink down into the grass and imagine that Otto was waiting for her by the river. This was a new delusion, and in her darkness she would lie for hours without moving. The Prut River flowed in fierce currents in that area, and its rapids were thrilling. More than once she said to herself, *I'll jump into the water and disappear.* But the desire to see Otto again drew her away from that desperate yearning. *To Vizhnitz,* she would repeat to herself, like a drowning man grasping a log.

Blanca imagined the way to Vizhnitz as a long, illuminated tunnel. At the beginning of it there was a ritual bath where people immersed themselves and were purified. After they were purified, they put on linen garments and advanced to the next stage. At the next stage they sat in a secluded area until their souls were emptied of their dross and they no longer remembered anything. From there the tunnel twisted and turned, but walking in it was not difficult.

One night Blanca found herself standing near a church. It was a village church, and two carved crucifixes stood in the courtyard. At first it seemed like a tranquil place, but then Blanca saw that the figures on the cross were not looking at her with affection. She was about to do what she had been in the habit of doing recently: slipping away. But this time, for some reason, her legs stopped her. She gathered some twigs and, without thinking about it, placed them next to the crucifixes. Then she lit a match and brought it close to the twigs. The twigs caught fire and raised a fine flame. She quickly stretched out her arms and warmed her cold hands.

For a long while Blanca stood and looked at the small fire, which gave off heat and a pleasant scent. The warmth seeped into her limbs, and her fingers and toes thawed out. Now she remembered her friend Sonia clearly, and how she had longed to go to her mother's hometown. Her strong face would soften when she spoke about Kolomyja, a place where she had never been. A few days ago Blanca had asked one of the peddlers whether Kolomyja was far away. He had given her a long and intricate answer, and then summed it all up by saying, "It's not far, but you'd be better off not putting yourself in danger during the winter. The winter is a time of troubles, and a person is better off if he sits at home and doesn't wander on the roads." Blanca stared at him, trying to absorb the meaning of his words. But the peddler's tired face expressed only the fatigue of his years. Blanca absorbed that fatigue more than his convoluted explanations.

Blanca added some more twigs, and the fire flared up again. Now the heat spread, and vapor rose from her damp clothes. For the first time after many days of wandering, a vision of Otto appeared before her. First it seemed to her that he was standing and looking out the window of the orphanage, as he used to do, but a second glance showed her that he had been forgotten on the balcony. He was asking for help, and no one was answering him. Blanca was so alarmed by the clarity of this vision that she didn't notice that the flames had spread to the figures on the crucifixes and had taken hold of them. With a quick movement she was about to remove the kerchief from her head and put out the fire, but her hands froze and she didn't do anything. The flames twisted up and embraced the crucifixes, quickly spread to the railing in front of the church, and from there climbed up to the doorpost and enveloped the beams. Blanca stepped back and then turned to go away. The night was dark and quiet, and the burning church lit up the sky. Only later, when the fire was already at its full strength, were the peasants called to help put it out.

"Fire has come down from heaven!" they shouted with dread. They tried to put out the fire, but it was too late.

That night Blanca found an abandoned barn and slept restfully there. When she awoke the next morning and remembered that she had set fire to the church, she wasn't frightened. It seemed to her that she had done an important thing and that from now on the roads would be open before her. Spite mingled with pleasure washed over her.

After another few days of wandering, Blanca set fire to another small church. Once again she gathered twigs and arranged them. The bonfire burned and warmed her hands. Then she watched as the fire spread and took hold of the church walls. This time the act of burning was accompanied not only by malicious pleasure but also by a kind of satisfaction; she had managed to deceive her pursuers, and from now on they would be busy putting out fires and not chasing after her.

And so Blanca continued to wander on that high plateau. The population was sparse, and only rarely would an abandoned horse or a lost cow emerge from the underbrush. Every time the desire to burn down a church arose in her, she would go and look for one. If she saw a church by daylight, she would say to herself, *Tonight I'll burn it down.* Now she did it without resentment or pleasure, but like a person obsessed.

Blanca met a Jewish peddler on the road, and in return for a gold ring she received from him a pair of galoshes and a long winter coat. The peddler was pleased, and so was Blanca. To his question about what a young Jewish woman was doing in these empty places, she hurriedly explained to him that she intended to get to Vizhnitz.

"If that's the case," he said, "you should take the King's Highway. The King's Highway is less dangerous."

He was wasting his words. Blanca was no longer frightened. Every church that she burned down boosted her courage. She stood up to the peasants, calling them wild men and worthless, and she looked at them with venom. If her expressions weren't effective, she would threaten them: *If you come near me, I'll choke you.* To herself she said: *If I overcome my fear of people, I won't fear death. I did what I did and had to do. From now on let God do His will. Otto won't judge his mother harshly.*

In her sleep, Blanca would see her mother and father; they were young, and their faces were full of youthful wonder. Their closeness to each other always seemed marvelous to her, and now she felt this even more strongly. Blanca believed that she would be reunited with them soon and that then the darkness would vanish. This brightened her spirits even more than the churches she burned down.

Between one rainstorm and the next Blanca would go down to the river, wash her feet, and wrap them in rags. Since she had bought the galoshes from the peddler, her sores had healed somewhat. If she came upon a church on her way, she would burn it down at night. She did it with diligence and attention, as though she were lighting the lanterns of Heimland.

Many sights were effaced from her memory, but not that of the church on Sundays: her father-in-law, her mother-in-law, and Adolf, and the kneeling and the pain that it caused her. On those crowded Sundays in the church and at the gatherings after it, parts of her soul would freeze. Now she felt that everything that had been paralyzed within her was throbbing with life again. *I did succeed at one thing,* she would console herself. *I excised Adolf from Otto's soul. If God helps me, his memory will be wiped out of the child's mind forever.*

Sometimes Blanca would enter a tavern, have a few drinks, and be thankful that the light of her eyes had not dimmed, that she could still walk on her two feet and make her way to Vizhnitz. It pained her that her father, whom she loved so much, had cut himself off from the tradition of his fathers and had no faith at all. Her life now, in these green hills where the houses were few and far between, seemed like just a link in a chain of events, each existing on its own but still joined together. *Dr. Nussbaum and Celia, Theresa and Sonia—I'll take them with me everywhere,* she kept repeating to herself. *Death isn't darkness if you take your dear ones with you. It's just a change in place. Innocence, simplicity, and devotion are great principles. So it is written in Buber's book,* The Hidden Light. *I will behave according to these principles until I reach the gates of light.*

Then the snowstorms began. Hunger and cold tormented her, but Blanca was cautious. Now she avoided entering taverns or the little railway stations that were scattered along her way. Posters about the

murderess were pasted on every public building—even on abandoned public buildings. Sometimes from a distance she would see
a squad of gendarmes searching the area or sitting on a hill, watching. In her heart she knew whom they were looking for.

Blanca wanted to stay alive and go back to see Otto. The thought
that perhaps one day she would be pardoned and go back to Struzhincz, and that Otto would stretch out his little arms and call out
"Mama!"—that thought was stronger than hunger, and it dragged
her legs from hill to hill.

Finally she had no choice. The cold gripped her fingers and
spread throughout her whole body. The pain was great. Blanca
entered a tavern, removed her wet coat and galoshes, and stood
next to the stove. She ordered a brandy and a sandwich. The bar-
tender prepared them for her. She sipped the drink and bit into the
sandwich. The brandy was strong, and she ordered another, and
then a third.

It was a peasant tavern, and long tables filled the dim room. A
few drunkards sat in the back of the room, cursing the empire and
the kaiser. The proprietor's warnings, that for curses like that people were sent to prison, were to no avail. The clamorous argument
didn't scare Blanca. The brandy set her head spinning, and before
her eyes she saw the churches she had set on fire. They had burned
for hours and lit up the night. She was sure that what she had done
had paved her way to Vizhnitz, which had until then been blocked.
Blanca approached the tavern owner, and to her surprise he spoke
German. He told her right away that he had served in the Austrian
army and that he had been stationed in Salzburg for years. Blanca
told him that she intended to go to Vizhnitz. Her ancestors had
gone on pilgrimages there, to ask the Tsadik for help.

"You don't look Jewish," he said, trying to flatter her.

"No?"

"The Jewish women in this region are suspicious and speak bad
German."

"All of them?"

"Most."

"I don't know how to pray, but I want to learn."

"The young Jews are moving away from the worship of God, if I'm not mistaken."

"You're right, it seems to me."

"A person with no God is a frightening creature," he said, twisting his lips.

"A person can't always find the path to God." Blanca tried to defend the accused.

"That's their parents' fault. The Jews are the captives of their children."

"You know Jews very well, I see." The irony of the old days came back to her.

"We know them very well." He spoke in the plural.

Strangely, that long conversation calmed her. It seemed to her that she had more time at her disposal, that she didn't have to hurry. Better to wait, to warm up, and to doze off a little.

At that moment the front door opened and two gendarmes walked in. They took off their hats and stepped up to the bar. Blanca opened her eyes and observed them with curiosity. The gendarmes were not young, and they sipped their drinks with enjoyment. They asked the tavern owner a few questions, and he explained to them at length that this time of year there were few customers, mostly poor people whose debts filled his books. They vomited and dirtied the floor, he said, and at night he was forced to drag them outside with his own hands.

"Don't you have any help?" the gendarmes asked in surprise.

"My late wife used to help me, but since she passed away, I do all the chores myself."

"Everybody has their own troubles." The gendarmes' sympathy was skin-deep.

Blanca was more and more fascinated by their conversation. As it happened, the gendarmes were Austrian. They had been sent there to advise the local police force. The tavern owner told them what he had just told Blanca, that in his youth he had served as a soldier in Salzburg, and that those had been the best years of his life. They spoke about the infantry and the artillery, recalling the camps and the well-known officers. They raised their glasses and cursed the winter that was seeping into their bones.

While the gendarmes were talking, Blanca realized they were speaking in the singsong accent of her hometown. That sound, so familiar, stunned her, and without hesitation she approached them.

"Is it not true that my ears have taken in the voices of Heimland?" she said.

"True, madam," answered the older gendarme.

"How long have you been here?"

"It's been a month already."

"I've been here longer. What's going on in my hometown?"

"Everything is as it was."

"It's good to see familiar people. Our accent gives us away immediately, does it not? Don't you miss home, too?"

"A little. What are you doing here?"

"I'm making my way to the Holy Rabbi of Vizhnitz. My parents of blessed memory were born in this region, and I'm following in their footsteps, to get the Holy Rabbi's blessing."

"Strange."

"Why strange?"

"In these times no one goes to holy men anymore."

"They are exalted men, sir. Have you never heard the name of Martin Buber?"

"No."

"He wrote a wonderful book about the faith of the Tsadiks."

The eyes of one of the gendarmes lit up.

"What's your name, if I may ask?"

"My name is Blanca Guttmann, and my father had a stationery store in Heimland."

"And you studied in the municipal high school?"

"Correct, sir."

"When, then, did you leave Heimland?"

"Right after my father's disappearance. My father lived during the last year of his life, or rather the last months of his life, in the old age home in Himmelburg, and he suddenly disappeared. God knows where he disappeared to. Since then I've been looking for him."

"How are you looking for him?"

"I go from place to place."

"And meanwhile you set churches on fire?"

"No, sir. That's strictly forbidden."

"I was suspicious of the innocent, apparently."

"I'm going straight to Vizhnitz from here. Maybe the Holy Rabbi will find the solution to his disappearance."

"Well, Stephan," the gendarme said, turning to his comrade, who had been standing silently at his side, "the fox has forgotten his tail."

Blanca didn't move or react to his words. She appeared to be caught up in the man's charm. The many drinks she had downed no longer made her dizzy. She stood on her two feet and placed her trust in those two gendarmes, who reminded her of the two old janitors in her high school. And when they placed handcuffs on her wrists and brought her to the police station, she neither complained nor pleaded.

"I used to go to My Corner with my father almost every week" was all that she said. "It's an excellent café, and its cheesecake is worthy of every praise. If there's one thing I miss now, it's a cup of coffee and their cheesecake. That's all, nothing more."